THE
SORROW
PROPER

THE
SORROW
PROPER

LINDSEY DRAGER

DZANC
BOOKS

DZANC BOOKS

5220 Dexter Ann Arbor Rd.
Ann Arbor, MI 48103
www.dzancbooks.org

Portions of this book have previously appeared in the following publications:

Redivider, as "Permutations"
Dislocate, as "Photographs I Did Not Take"
Web Conjunctions, as "Toward a General Theory of Distance"
Artifice Magazine, as "A Statistical Analysis of the Library Prior to Its Being Emptied: A Briefing"

Designed by Steven Seighman

Library of Congress Cataloging-in-Publication Data

Drager, Lindsey.
  The sorrow proper : a novel / Lindsey Drager.
    pages cm
  ISBN 978-1-938103-00-1 1. Life change events—Fiction. 2.
  Social change—Fiction. I. Title.
  PS3604.R335S68 2015   813'.6—dc23

                                    2014041162

First U.S. Edition: April 2015

Printed in the United States of America

10   9   8   7   6   5   4   3   2   1

CONTENTS

The absence of eternity is not simply a limit that is thought, but a lack that is felt at the heart of temporal experience. The limiting idea then becomes the sorrow proper to the negative.

—Paul Ricoeur, *Time and Narrative*

I

THE ART OF CIRCULATION

THE LIBRARY MAY CLOSE. The women who work there are told at the end of the day and as it begins to rain. The hair has fallen out of the bottoms of their weak buns and their pocketbooks are tight against their sides. When they are told, they do not hold their hands to their lips. They look down at the path of worn carpet or up at the ceiling's spots of mold. One of them says, *Shit*.

In the parking lot, the rain staining their cardigans dark, they decide to get a drink.

What Genevieve can't figure out, she tells the others, wiping beer foam from above her lip with her sleeve, is what will happen to all the books. *All those shelves and shelves of books*, she says, and no one looks at anyone else. All that time they had so carefully recorded. All that noise they'd been so diligent to hush.

Mercedes puts her glass down too hard and everyone looks at her, waiting for retort. But she murmurs an apology and brushes the hair from her face.

Avis wants to know why.

It might be because of the Bronson girl last year, Genevieve tells her glass.

No, Harriet says definitively, *a company can't be responsible for what happens on the street in front of it.*

Is a library a company? Mercedes asks, and they look at her with their best *Be Quiet* faces, and then they all look at their hands.

For a long while they are silent, thinking about abstract things like control and what it means to love an institution that is defined by loss, because the library is such a space and their duty is to encourage the books to leave. They briefly debate ordering another round and then give in and discuss the way they feel the covers with their palms and finger the spines lightly before they stamp the cards and how their breath quickens a bit when a book exits the glass front doors because they know it might not be coming back, or that when it does it may be in poorer condition because so many value the book as a catalyst for thought and not as an artifact. Their eyes grow wide and start to gloss from tears when they voice the saddest cases, which they decide unanimously are those involving water damage. They toast to these and loudly clear their throats.

When the women leave that night they look at each other without smiling, then at the way the water that lies on the road reflects the headlights of oncoming traffic, casting shine in their bifocal lenses. When each woman reaches her respective home, she locks her door and slips between the covers by herself. And as they lie in bed, they consider what it would look like, the library emptied, and think about the things that make them sad, all of which boil down to lack: a lost mitten nestled between chairs in the Children's Wing, the unlit cigarettes that are dropped just before the large front door, the walls with abandoned hooks left by the local photographer after he dismantles his exhibits.

They think about void, the emptiness of that era between lying down in bed and falling asleep, how it passes differently than the rest of time. They think there is only one other space in which time moves like that, without reflecting progress, a kind of eddying shift, and as they consider this, they each shake their heads and look up, the universal attempt to fight gravity when one feels grief moving in.

They are thinking of the blank pages between the end of the story and when the cover comes.

THE PHOTOGRAPHER FINDS HIMSELF taking down his photos just a week after putting them up. This is how long the library allows him to feature his exhibits since he is not yet established in his field. He uses a small ladder and removes each frame from the wall. There is a woman standing in front of the frame farthest from him, looking closely, brow furrowed and biting her nails. The photographer takes his time to shift the ladder six feet to the left, and then confirms it is sound before taking a cautious step. He holds both ends of each wide frame and lifts directly up, then forward, before slowly stepping back down. He does this thirty-one times with thirty-one frames until he reaches the woman, still standing in front of the last. He steps out for a cigarette, hoping this will give her time to leave, but when he returns, she is standing there still.

Excuse me, he tells her back, and when she doesn't move he touches her on the shoulder with his full hand.

The woman turns around and when she faces him, smiles. The photographer starts to tell her he is taking the photos down, but she shakes her head and points to her ears, the wide grin still spanning her face. Her eyes return to the wall.

The exhibit chronicled a collection of wine glasses, all with lipstick stains on the brims, most with chips and only one that is not empty. The glasses are thin and tall or broad and deep, with or without stems. They are standing up or stacked unevenly together or lying on their sides. They are all situated somewhere in a bathroom, lying on the drain of the sink or standing next to the soap on a shelf, stem up on the lip of the tub or hanging dangerously from the towel rack. Only the last photograph shows wine and there is no lipstick stain and it is standing on the toilet seat.

The photographer wants to go home. He would like to be in his darkroom, spending the five minutes that are required for the eyes to adjust to confirm all the light is bound. He touches her on the shoulder again and when she turns around she looks almost surprised that he is still there. She digs into her purse and pulls something thin from the mess of her hair, hands him the pen and the pad of paper.

The exhibit is over

he writes, and hands it back. Over the speaker he can hear a soft voice telling the patrons that it is time to go, *You have fifteen minutes to make your choices and make your way up front.*

She tears the sheet off and hands him her response:

The glass: half empty or full?

He looks up from the pad and she nods her head curtly toward the wall.

He looks at his photo, stares hard at the glass balanced on the curved lid of the toilet seat. His eyes follow the grid of the print, scanning, and he notices something he hadn't before; a bobby pin sitting in the crack of the tile in the bottom left corner of the shot.

7

He looks at the ground and then shyly tilts his head in her direction, squints his eyes.

There is a moment when he almost thinks to leave.

He holds up the pad with two hands, taps his finger against the text.

The exhibit is over

She nods and flattens her lips, makes an audible *hmm*.

I collect spoons

she writes, and his eyebrows lift. She raises her index finger and draws the frame of a spoon in the air. Then she pulls it from where it is suspended, licks the cove, and places it on her nose.

He grunts a laugh and shakes his head at the ground, fighting the smile that develops somewhere in his cheeks. The woman flips the pad to a page where the following words are already written:

Do you want to hear a joke?

She helps him wrap all thirty-two frames in newspaper. He cringes at the sound of the paper's crunch, feeling guilty for disturbing the silence that defines a library, but it doesn't bother her. He works quickly out of haste, and the announcements, *Ten minutes, Five minutes, Please make your choices and make your way up front*, make him increasingly anxious for what reason he doesn't know. If nothing else, there would always be tomorrow.

She helps him carry the wrapped frames to his car. After the last haul, they both head in once more. *Sorry about the noise,* he tells the librarians, who are sitting behind the long front desk that curves like a coast. All the women have their feet up, skirts wrapped tightly around their legs so nothing is exposed. They don't look at him when they speak and the photographer thinks he sees a wide but slender bottle being passed beneath the volume of their skirts. They tell him that the library isn't condemned to silence anymore, given the building's potential fate. Then one of them stands up on her chair and yells *Time's up! Get out!* but there is no one left to hear and the echo dies young. The photographer smiles weakly at the librarians, who start to put on their coats and talk in low tones about what they'll drink tonight.

The library is closing

he writes on the paper, perhaps to soothe the atmosphere. Or perhaps to invite the woman to exercise shared sympathy with him.

She reads the note and looks at the grand clock that stands above the exit sign.

I know

the pad reads.

IN TIMES BEFORE, WHEN the photographer would write on her body, he admired the way it lingered for days, fading slowly, working toward erase. The night before he finds the deaf mathematician in the bathtub, he will uncap the black marker and watch the skin dip where the pressure of the tip sits. He will watch the ink split and turn in jagged paths at the borders of each mark, settling into the clefts between the discs of her skin. It will look like a miniscule branching. The sentence will run from the inside of her thigh up and around the thick of her rear and end in the small of her back.

And then, in the bathroom, before the gravity of event weighs in, before he has time to consider what he will do with her spoons and her debt, he will think he should scrub the dirty words away, save them both from being the joke of the men who will see her like this, the story they tell their colleagues after work, over drinks, that ends in wide grins and hung heads. He thinks about the way that if he does not move now, what should be temporary will set and sit as fact.

A note on trajectory: things either intersect, refract, or pass untouched.

When the men come to take her away he is not scrubbing; he is stroking her matted hair. The photographer sees it in their faces—that they, too, have practiced the act of marker and skin, and words have coiled ascending from their lovers' legs and trunks, and they stare back into his eyes and tell him he should not look when they lift because the body will not be limp.

In the paper the next day, they spell her name wrong.

THE PHOTOGRAPHER SPREADS OUT the deaf mathematician's spoons on the living room floor. He starts to organize them by size and then by condition, angle of bend, degree of rust. She descends the stairs with two mugs and places them on the cold cement floor before sitting down.

He has refused to photograph her. When she probes him for a reason, he presses hard on the pad. *A photo is "taken,"* he scribes, *a subject is "captured." Photography is violent and cruel.*

But now, after studying him during these first few weeks together, she believes it's because he simply would not know how. He would not know which angle, how close to focus in or what to focus on. He wouldn't know what to abandon with frame, which parts of her were worth leaving outside of still life, how to translate her body to the flat plane of matte finish. She suspects he would not be able to drown her in the stop bath, let her sit in the dark of the basement for hours alone. She knows he could never care about her in that form after she was developed, could not imagine her so carefully and cautiously reduced.

Mostly, though, she knows he believes a photo of her *is* her, not just organized light that tells a transient story. And she knows, she thinks, watching him stack her spoons, watching the deep worry lines span his face, that he would never condense her to photo when he could have her as flesh and bone.

He is trying to pose the spoons in something resembling order but he can't find a shot that reveals anything to him. He puts the coves up or down, stacks them together or profiles each one alone. He takes shots from above or the side, featuring the tiny scratches in the dip or the engravings on the base, the relationship of the width of the mouth to the length of the handle. He only gets one that he believes speaks; a profile featuring the spoon's arc, so that the thesis of the image is the background, which contains a blurry image of her empty chair, a blanket folded modestly on top.

She watches him for longer than she'd care to recall while her students' papers sit unmarked. She watches him until he sits back in frustration and packs his cigarettes hard.

She pulls out her notebook and writes:

Try this

and she picks up a handful of her spoons, ruining their calculated position, the angles achieved and the poses enforced. She holds them up in the air so that her arm is perpendicular to the length of her body and before he can object she drops them. They fall too quickly for the eye to detect; they are in her hands, and then they are splayed across the floor.

The photographer rises and starts to assess the scene and the deaf mathematician sits back down, finally uncapping her pen.

Days later, when he is clipping the photos to the line, he will have to sit because they are so haunting, so rich and succinct, displaying a tenor he hasn't been able to reach. And as he sits there in her chair, looking at the line depicting her felled spoons, he

13

can't help feeling close to her in a way he can't get when she is in the room. Maybe it is knowing that a particular kind of care is involved in the act of photographing another's personal effects, and that he has now inextricably linked his affection for her with his work. Maybe it is the fact that he knows her spoons will outlive her, operate as cast, as proof that she once was.

Or maybe, he thinks, spotting a spoon that skirted its way under his cropping board, it is knowing that theory is easier to love.

THE PHOTOGRAPHER IS ILL. The deaf mathematician takes off work and sits next to him in bed for hours as he sleeps. She grades papers in red ink, puts tiny stars next to each question answered correctly.

At one point, she glances over at him to study his hands. When he was young, before he knew what pain was, his father broke a mirror and the child held the pieces of glass in his hands. When he made fists, the mirror entered his palms and fingertip pads. The deaf mathematician thinks of the photographer in this way often, his tiny hands gripping the glass so that he might see his reflection, perhaps for the first time. And then the rush of red and how, with a wound like that, pain isn't felt at first. How for a moment he might have recognized that there was a world inside of him that he hadn't known about. Then, she thinks each time she thinks of this, how the knowledge of pain hit and this was the first union of body and mind. How he signaled his hurt with a howl and then his parents came in to hold him and begin to close the wounds.

She studies the scars now, which are thin and raised. She notices the way the skin curves and twists in an attempt to suture itself, to close the gaps it knows should not exist. She sees how the long lines on the inside of his palms break often for scar.

Hands will become tools to him, she thinks, *if this thing between us lasts.* He is already starting to sign; HELLO, GOODBYE, PLEASE, DRINKS? and LET'S GO TO BED.

How sad, she thinks, touching his hands now, fingering the marks where glass once stood in a time that is as foreign to him as to her, *when the hands become the mode for thought instead of simple limbs.* She has never known them as anything other, and she lets her eyes shift from his to her own, the nails clipped close, the pads stained with ink, the pattern of tiny hairs that peeks from the pores between the knuckle bends.

He stirs then, because she has stopped stroking his hands, and when his eyes open he sneezes, then smiles.

I will need you exactly always

she writes on the pad that they keep on the table by the bed.

He looks up at her wide eyes and instead of objecting, stretches his neck to kiss her forehead, then rolls over to fall back asleep.

It would be impossible to tell her, he thinks, that in no world is always ever exact.

WHAT IS COLLECTED TURNS cruel. When she draws her baths, she does it with one hand in the pooling tub. When she draws her drapes, she does it with one hand on the gathering folds. In the mornings, the photographer would wake her by fingering the cove of her navel. Now she finds herself waking in the middle of the night, doing it to herself.

The deaf mathematician sits in her car at the landfill of bodies. She is not smoking or biting her nails. She is not touching her lips or tightening her thighs. Her head is not at a tilt. She watches the snow fall, thinks of her failed proofs, the negatives he never threw away. She wants to develop them, is willing to empty the frames that line the borders of the house now, but she cannot pull them from the walls. To touch would mean a violation. To change what was set would be participating in his end. Now, in the car at the place where under the soil her lover's body is set and settling, she looks at her hands. Under the soil his body sinks, the skin around the fingernails shrinking so that the nail seems to extend. It is a trick of the eye, the moving back. The tractor's mouth opens, the lazy jaw draws back and bites the earth above the photographer's plot, and it begins to flurry and once, when he was writing a dirty message on her thigh in black ink, he told his deaf mathematician that the sound of snow falling is one that she knows.

That evening, when she is home and the snow lies dormant over everything flat, she lets her hand hesitate over a bottle of wine, grabs instead champagne and sits in front of her equations to celebrate the ceremony of repeal.

On Thursdays craft beer is half price, so tonight the librarians drink stouts and porters instead of cheap lager. They talk about the people they will no longer see when the library closes. They talk about the thesis of mourning, and the meaning of loss, the way the books will be stripped slowly so that at first the patrons will not be able to tell. They talk about the photos that hang on the far west wall.

How long do you think it will take? Genevieve asks.

It will be slow, Harriet says. *A library is a hard thing to kill. The numbers say three years.*

A three-year sentence on death row, Avis says, taking a drink. She nods while she swallows. *There is something to say for the Band-Aid method.*

Genevieve raises her glass. All four grunt agreements and take another swig.

You know that eventually they're going to ask us to leave, Avis says, running her hand down the length of the tabletop.

Yes, Harriet says. *Which is why the time for action is now.*

Avis is looking out the window. She nods in small bobs at nothing, so that Harriet thinks she might be starting to shake. Avis does not turn when Harriet clears her throat.

Look, Avis. Harriet says. They are all concerned about Avis, they each think then. Since the accident, she has grown more passive, her stare hardened, her voice lower. They have watched the features of her face grow more angular and her eyes have gone flat. They make mention of this in brief moments when they are alone, when Avis does checks in the silent rooms to confirm they aren't being abused by eager high school couples. *Avis,* Harriet says more gently, and finally Avis looks. *These are simply the terms under which we are working. If we want to save the library, we have to amend.* Harriet rolls her mug between her flattened hands so that her wedding ring makes a rhythmic clicking against the glass.

Avis catches a flock of birds moving low in the sky, casting shadow over the street. *The matter is more a question of to save or to preserve,* she says, and lifts her mug to her lips.

Genevieve gives a loud huff and Harriet shoots her a sharp glance. *Would you rather be a hero or a martyr?* Genevieve says, pushing the hair from her forehead and pulling her cardigan close.

Yes, Mercedes tells the tabletop. *Yes, it's true,* she says. *When you're looking down the barrel of a gun, you have a certain responsibility to make sure the thing is loaded.*

Everyone looks at Mercedes, who fixes the pleats on her skirt. Harriet catches the waiter and orders another round.

They are sitting at the tall circular table in the window in the front of the bar. Because it is growing colder, there are fewer people to watch, but still Avis looks outside when she speaks. *What about a coffee stand,* she says. She notices a thin border of condensation forming in the window frame.

Yes, Harriet says, setting the shot glass down. *We could have a little stand with a few tables and then people could sit out there and read.* Here Harriet looks at Genevieve, who encourages her with a nod. *They did it at the Carlsberg branch and it seemed to catch on.*

All the women sit quietly. They finger the rims of their pints and look up at the ceiling or down at the table, riddled with graffiti on a horizontal plane.

We would have to lose some books, to make room, Avis articulates, to make sure they understand.

We have doubles of most of the classics, Genevieve says, *and the magazines could be purged.*

That night, before they go to bed, they will each flip through a book, find themselves unable to read the words. They will think that this is distance, growing further away from what sits unchanging in the palm of the hand. They will think of the thin shells of hard cover they collected when they were small, in that time before they knew what the black code meant, in a time when the only way to read a book was to flip each paper page.

Now Avis watches the birds settle like a dark sheet over the street and building tops. She looks across the bar's table at each of her colleagues; Genevieve eager, optimistic, Harriet bold and reserved, and Mercedes, the last to be hired, the youngest by far, quiet and gloomy, the hair at her temples just starting to go grey. Avis bends her chest across the table so they all have to lean in close to listen. She shakes her head and closes her eyes. *You know where this is headed,* Avis says. She stays that way for a moment, hovering across the table, allowing the words to settle in their minds.

Mercedes fingers the letters carved into the tabletop. They feel like the titles engraved in the covers of old books. The tip of her finger follows the dip of the words, which read,

EVEN STARS DIE.

THE DEAF MATHEMATICIAN AND the photographer are lying in bed. The deaf mathematician signs to him *Bed* and he signs back. When she signs to him *Bedroom*, he tries to mimic her but grows frustrated and grabs the notebook from the bedside table.

Can't we just write forever?

He raises his eyebrows. She flips the paper over.

How will we ever fight?

He was embarrassed when he asked her why she couldn't read lips. *Because it's hard*, she had written, laughing. And then she'd asked, *Why can't you?*

He picks up her pillow, tosses it a few times and lays it back down, using his hands to make it smooth. She makes a low-pitched wail and he starts, asks her in sign, *What?*

She points to his pillow, the cove from where his head rested the night before. She fingers the outline of his imprint, pats the air above it gently with her palm, leaving the dent undisturbed.

She grabs the pad and pulls a pen from her hair.

This is how I have you even when you're gone.

She looks at him when she hands it back. She touches the words with her finger, drags it under the sentence, tapping the last word twice. Finally his eyes rise from the notebook to her face, then the bed, disheveled, sheets caught in coil, covers with no beginning or end.

He takes a deep breath, the pen hovering over the page.

Okay

he writes, then hesitates:

But can I make your side?

WHAT IS MOVING IS her want. If asked, she would say that want is a measure of feeling, a root cellar full of wine. She is done with wine but liked the process of opening it, the screw twisting and in twisting entering the cork, the way it is worked out slowly and steadily, until the empty mouth is exposed. Now she drinks only champagne, unclasps the thin metal strips that hold the cork in place, uses her thumb to work it out. It is less the taste than the meaning she finds in opening the bottle, the suspense in waiting for the moment of detonation. She is powerless to know when the pop will strike and this lesson in disclosure is enough to keep her still bathing, still waiting for the mail to come.

As she drinks, she thinks of the ways her body moves without consent. Once, they sat watching her thigh spasm, but each silently, alone, wondering what prompts such movement. Along the bottom of the screen the closed captioning slid, capturing the action above, but they did not look. They watched the thigh, which touched her calf because of the fold of her leg, until its movement ceased and even a few moments after, and without looking at one another simultaneously returned their gazes to the screen.

A stop bath sits in a dark room, waiting to rinse prints clean. In the bathtub, smudges from her fingers line the lip. A bath is not a filled cup anymore. It is a failed apparatus. It is a broken system.

OFTEN, WHILE THE PHOTOGRAPHER is working in the basement, the deaf mathematician takes walks to the library to look at his exhibits. He does not know she does this and she prefers it this way. When they look at his work together, he is intent on study—the angle of the shot, the crop of the frame, the balance of dark and light—when all she wants to do is admire.

She stands in front of his framed photos one at a time. He is careful to establish a narrative, a singular story the images tell. She looks at each frame for a stretch of time that the librarians deem too long before she shuffles three feet to the left. Her head is not at a tilt. Her hand is not on her hip.

This exhibit contains corkscrews. They range from the tiny hinged tools from Swiss Army knives to an intricate bulk of metal and plastic with wings. The exhibit starts with screws alone—then there is a picture of two on polar sides of the frame, then two that have their coils caught. There are screws with corks still stuck on their length and one in which the spiral is broken off. There is a line of screws with dull tips that all end pointing left, a close-up of a thin cylinder set inside a larger one so that the wooden hand pieces stand in opposition. The deaf mathematician makes her way to the end, staring hard at each frame and hesitating before she moves on, as though afraid that if her eyes lingered elsewhere, the images would move. When she gets to the final frame, she learns the story's conclusion; there is a screw stuck in the cork of an empty bottle that stands in a mess of the contents it once held, a pin-thin crack traversing the bottle's length.

If the institution of mathematics told a story, she thinks then, wanting to touch the photo, feel the cold glass on her hand, how would it end?

She will think of this on nights he falls asleep before her, when she's composing her proofs in bed, the wine bottle shut tight, the skin of glass split, the firm hold of the screw. And one night this will be the key to solving the rest of her proof.

Later, when he asks her to translate what it means, she will reduce her eighty-six pages of sound equation to the realm of story. She will write it down on paper and he'll tape it to his darkroom wall.

Procedure follows this law: It doesn't matter
how much damage there is.
If the right part fails, expect collapse.

27

After the blinds are drawn, the librarians do not gather their coats. Instead, they separate and circle the library looking for the books with the saddest histories.

The library contains one copy of *Moby-Dick*, the cover of which has been vandalized so that there is no longer an "o" or "b". Most of Beckett's books have pages dog-eared and Calvino's *Collected Stories* is riddled in red pen. The final page of *Frankenstein* is gone. Others have coffee rings or tears, spines so broken the glue chips off. Without speaking, Mercedes and Avis pull these off the shelf and cart them to the front. Harriet and Genevieve disengage the tiny pads that will sound the alarm with a tool they once agreed felt like a gun. Then all four of them carefully put the books in the tote bags that read PUBLIC LIBRARY, slip unnoticed through the detectors, and lock the front doors.

They carry the books to their cars and hide them in their trunks.

That night, at the bar, they discuss how to find meaning in a life that cares for books. They talk about the rise of the computer and the death of the Dewey decimal system; best-sellers lists and trade paperback. They debate the meaning of their work.

All we do is catalogue and shelve, catalogue and shelve. What have we done with the years, other than perfected the art of circulation? Mercedes asks.

Don't do that, Mercedes, Genevieve says. *Don't do that to yourself. We do more than just care for books. We encourage the act of reading. We promote the distribution of knowledge.*

Avis waves to the bartender and reminds them all that library care is a harnessed technique and that they are happy—aren't they?—except with the state of the books.

A library is not a museum, Harriet says, and is sure to look them all in the eye.

Nor is it a store, Genevieve tells her, and Harriet looks away, runs an empty shot glass back and forth between her flat palms.

One day things will change, Mercedes says, taking a tentative sip.

But Genevieve isn't sure. She has known what it means to wait, knows well the danger of simply killing time. *Do you know what that's called? Repeating the same behavior and expecting different results?* She uses her palm to push her thin bangs from her eyes, leaves the hand on her head. She tells them that is what it means to be insane.

The women put their drinks down on the table and look in all directions except at each other.

You're wrong, Avis tells Genevieve, her head bobbing slightly, her swollen fingers gripping the edge of the tabletop. *That's the principle of progress, the notion that things will one day change. We must expect different results, otherwise the whole world becomes petrified.* Avis sits up a bit in her chair. She downs the rest of her beer in one swig and reminds them all about the Bronson family, the parents of the little girl who died in front of the library last year. That they continue to make their beds and tie their shoes and watch it rain but they are hoping for a day that provides different results. Harriet puts her shot glass down and Mercedes stops biting her lip. That is the thesis of grief, she tells them, and at the end of the day, isn't that what we spend our lives doing? Grieving for the past, or the future, grieving for the people and the places, the ideas we do not have, whether we once did or never will. *If expecting different results makes us crazy, then we are all insane,* Avis says. *That's what keeps the whole world moving: the suspense of different results.*

Then there is only the sound of breathing. There is the sound of shifting chairs and legs being recrossed. There is the sound of a zipper to a pocketbook opening with the intent of buying another drink. Mostly there is the sound of resolve.

I think the photographer is in love with the deaf woman, Genevieve says finally.

Mercedes fingers the lip of her mug. *How can you tell?*

He touches her the way we touch the books.

II

WHAT IS UNTHIRST?

ONCE A WEEK THE photographer and the deaf mathematician walk to the local theater to watch a silent film. They put four dollars under the Plexiglas face of the one-man stand in the center of the grand front doors. They put their coats on the rack in the lobby. They put themselves in seats toward the back.

Tonight they watch the story of a scientist whose lover cannot arouse her. She spends years in her laboratory trying to develop a serum to wake her body, to make her move in ways that he can spark. She becomes obsessed with cracking her own secret code, reduces her body to equation to solve. Years pass this way and they grow old and apart. There is a melodramatic scene in which she sits in her lab, surrounded by proofs and maps of her body's terrain. She looks out the window at her lover walking away. The text on the screen reads:

Is it that I am woman or scientist that condemns me to feel close to him only when I am alone?

On their way out, the photographer and the deaf mathematician hold hands. They traverse the street and head straight to a dark tavern, the oldest bar in town. The lights are down and there is frost or steam, something cloudy and white, softly framing the large window. The deaf mathematician can't make out the shape of those at the table in the window until just before she and the photographer reach the sidewalk to turn left.

Inside the bar the librarians are talking loudly and at the same time. They are debating whether or not they should implement an ongoing book sale in one of the silent rooms. It will happen, and when weeks later the deaf mathematician enters the doors to see people lined up for the sale, the smell of coffee brewing from the back, she will notice the faces of the library staff, how they look empty and defeated, though she has not seen so many people in the library for years.

But here in the bar, nothing is set and everyone has an opinion except for Mercedes. Something outside the window moves and catches her glance.

The deaf mathematician and Mercedes lock eyes. Before they look away, Mercedes raises her glass.

For the rest of the way home, the deaf mathematician thinks of the way the librarians looked circled around the table, their faces wrought with passion, their mugs half empty of beer; how they probably went home each night to dripping faucets and lovers who did not hold them; how the moment she looked away became static, all the women in profile, mouths open and sleeves rolled up; how the scene was like a photo, framed in the window, and if it were and she had to crop it, what would she be willing to lose?

After the rain, everything that is vessel is filled. And even that which is not vessel is filled; the weight of the water makes tarps that were once taut now dip, the concrete path's invisible arcs now clear. The birds that have not yet hit the windows of the library drink from the puddles where the water is opaque.

Lately she forgets things, finds herself parked in strange driveways, practices pause and search when it comes to spelling her name. When she goes out, she has to remind herself to trust: her feet not to slip, the buildings not to fall. She begins to notice the things men do with their hands; stroking their palms, the thick of their knuckles, correcting their groins and their beards, pulling bobby pins from breast pockets and absently fingering them, using the thumb tip to split the pin's legs.

She only drinks champagne now and is forgetting the most basic calculations. In the bath, she performs the times tables to keep her mind sharp, rests her full glass on the tub's lip, is careful not to touch where he last set his bar of soap. When the deaf mathematician steps up and out of the tub, she untapes the bandages around her leg and pulls them back to reveal the words he wrote in ink on her skin. If asked, she would say these are the things one does to defend against the linear; if the world resists preservation, we must slow change down.

His bar of soap is growing cracks, she notices; there are sweat pills on her glass. It is a terrible kind of awe, the deaf mathematician thinks, sinking naked to the tiled bathroom floor, understanding the power of that which goes unseen.

THE DEAF MATHEMATICIAN AND the photographer are sitting on the porch of his house while outside the rain falls hard. They hold two mugs of coffee and stare at the falling rain. She pulls her legs to her chest and her arms inside her shirt, sets her mug between her knees. She stares at the rain until she catches the wave of his hand.

Your thought, he signs to her, and then supplements with the notepad:

What's going on in that head?

She smiles at him and takes a deep breath, looks back out at the rain. She signs something but it is too complex. He shakes his head and points to the paper pad. She resists, spells her name, then the word *house*, nodding to the front door, and then signs *together*.

Weeks later, after they haul all her boxes upstairs, he'll take a break to smoke in the backyard and she'll explore the contours of his attic, find one of his retired cameras in a box of his documents. She will study it, feel its heft in her hands, wrap the strap around her neck, peek through the lens to enter the space he has lived in for years. The camera, she knows, is more than his tool; it is his source of grounding. It is the mechanism through which he organizes the world; there is everything he has not photographed, and then the things he has. Everything he captures through camera is bound forever in light, stuck eternally in the past. She looks closely at the places where the oils from his skin have left behind fingerprints. She thinks briefly: the prints these fingers left are not those of the man she sees now outside, running two palms down his back, cigarette hanging from his lips. Right before the press, she will hesitate, consider what he has told her: that once the camera captures, it is an end. She'll hold the camera steady, considering. She will feel the shutter, then she'll see the flash.

But before this, here and now on the porch, he smiles at the proposition, reaches out for her hand and they both squeeze and hold. She can feel the raised scars on his palms, the hard of his knuckles, the rough skin of his fingertips. But when he tries to study her hands, all he feels is cold.

They stay this way for a while and he thinks about the right amount of time lapse before he should release, tries to feel her out, to get the sense of when it should be done.

And then, without warning, she lets go.

WHEN THE PHOTOGRAPHER GETS the call from the gallery, he is at the kitchen table cropping shots. The phone rings and she sees the blinking light. He reaches for it without looking up, puts it to his ear. She watches him hold the mouthpiece between his head and shoulder, bent over his photos, still measuring and making marks. He is working on a new project—coasters—the thesis being the wet ring left behind, how it lasts for a particular period before it disappears. She watches him drop the uncapped marker and stand up. He signs to her, *finally*, and she opens two dark beers.

To celebrate, they have dinner outside in the front yard under their favorite tree.

What do you think you'll exhibit? the deaf mathematician asks.

The photographer takes another drink of his beer. He puts his bottle down to respond. *I don't know.*

She can't remember him smiling like this before, not even in those first months after they met.

She tears him off more bread and he takes it from her hand with his teeth, signs, *A full hall for three weeks,* grabs it from his mouth. She sets her thumb in the dip of his chin.

While he eats, she sips her beer and thinks about her proofs, wonders when she'll have news for him like this.

He already knows he'll use her spoons, but doesn't tell her then. When weeks later they enter the empty wing, just the two of them, holding hands, the gallery curator will watch them walk the long hall back and forth, stare at the blank walls like there is something there. The curator will watch them in awe, this couple smiling at nothing, pointing to it, looking at each other as though those empty walls are full of the rest of their lives.

IN THE CLASSROOM, STANDING in front of her blank-face students, the deaf mathematician loses her train of thought. In doing so, she thinks of this idiom, how false it is that thought follows a path like the tracks of a train. Or maybe not; train tracks split and meet again later, some tracks run parallel and never meet. And tracks end abruptly, are left unfinished or are abandoned and grown over with brush, get buried with time.

She puts her hand to her forehead to block the light and scans the room. How many of them have walked tracks at night, put toe to heel on the raised metal, felt sound coming through the ties? It is a feeling that resides in that twilight space of language somewhere between a shudder and a shake.

I'm sorry, the deaf mathematician signs and her students blink blankly. *Where were we?*

Three students sign back to her, *Valid vs. sound*, and her thought returns to its place. She says that for an argument to be sound, it must be valid, but also, the premises must be true; if the first premise is false, then the argument is not sound.

Then she puts two premises and a conclusion on the board.

All mortals die.
I am mortal.
Therefore, I will die.

Once, one of her students objected. This was in her first year of teaching and she'd not been prepared for debate. Math, she had thought, was a discipline of fact; there was no room for belief. Things either were or were not.

If the premises must be true, the student had asked, *then we have to know the first is not false.* She had looked at him perplexed. *How do you know all mortals die?* the student asked. The room had gone still.

She had thought for a moment, wondered how to navigate this. In later years, she would be prepared, explain the divorce between theory and practice, describe the split between experiment and law. But there, a young mathematician without much experience in how to relay these ideas in writing or signs, to lovers or kids, had pulled her hands to her chest and told them she didn't know. She told them she did not know and that it was okay, that part of math is trust.

For years she had debated whether or not she had meant it, this rule she had taught her first class. It had pacified them and they had gone on with the lesson, but often she'd spent time thinking about whether she believed it herself.

This class doesn't object. They are clear about mortals and death.

This is both valid and sound, her most attentive student responds. They've started working on his application for a scholarship she's sure he'll receive. The deaf mathematician nods in return.

She tells them to try another and writes this on the board:

All organisms with wings can fly.
Penguins have wings.
Therefore, penguins can fly.

A student in the back whose parents just divorced explains that while the argument is valid, it is not sound, as penguins cannot fly.

She asks if they might come up with another example. A student who always sits as close to her as possible raises his hand. He has recently left home, moved in with his older brother. He is now getting better grades. The deaf mathematician calls on him by name.

All humans with ears can hear, the student signs.

Later, when she gets home, she'll explain this scene to the photographer. Be lucky you do not teach literature, he will tell her. Be lucky you do not have to profess about a speaker, an audience, voice. Even the word language comes from the Latin for "tongue," he will tell her. There's just no escaping the idea that word derives from the mouth.

The deaf mathematician's hands are wet and the chalk that cakes them is a paste. It feels like a long walk to the board. She records the premise and stays there for a moment, her back to the class, collecting herself. Then she asks, *What's next?*

A girl who has never participated in class before, a girl the deaf mathematician has talked to many times in conferences about her lack of participation, raises her hand. The girl is not passive or uninterested, but nervous, she had explained, that she'd get the answer wrong.

We have ears

the young girl says. The deaf mathematician keeps herself steady. She writes the premise slowly and clearly underneath the first. She turns around and tells her class, *therefore...*

The entire class signs back to her, simultaneously, the same three words.

We can hear.

43

The class is quiet then, taking notes and thinking to themselves, pointing to each other's script to clarify the rule. They will take down the argument and forget it, she thinks, rolling the chalk between her fingers, the dust getting caught under her nails. She circles the room and catches a glimpse of one of her students' notebooks.

On the margin at the top of the page, above the equation sitting on the board, the boy has written in capital letters and underlined twice:

THIS IS NOT SOUND

SHE POINTED ONCE TO his single shelf of books and called it a library, more a declaration than a christening. How, he wonders, can that sad and small collection share a name with the great building that will soon stand gaping, front doors open like loose lips?

She was best when wet, just out of the tub, pores raised and red, or at night when she woke from bad dreams and thick coils of hair adhered to her damp forehead. These were the times she needed him most, he thinks now, pulling the frames from the wall. He will empty them, discard the photographs of her spoons. He will put the frames back up, careful that each is returned to its same position, so that they frame nothing, stand as voids for him to fill and refill with everything that did not happen, with all the things that could and that he feels are happening now, though elsewhere, somewhere he can't get because of the mandates of distance.

The frames that line the walls of the house are as vacant as the bathtub, empty and yawning. It is not that they are unfull, for in their emptiness they possess the property to contain all possibility, the way a finger pointing with particular aim too far from the goal in effect points to everything.

Once she tricked him.

It happened on their way home from watching a silent film in which someone was kidnapped in a driveway. On the walk from the car to the front door, she raised her arm suddenly, halting him mid-stride.

Did you hear that? she asked.

Hear what? he replied with his hands.

No birds hit the windows the day Genevieve cancels all the subscriptions. She spends the whole day on the phone, apologizing to each publication, and she does not break for lunch. As they begin to close, they notice her pull up a stool to the magazine and journal stacks, flip through them absently, touching the cover of each.

At the bar, they talk about what they've lost.

A book deal, Harriet says.

You wrote a book? Avis asks.

Harriet nods, holding the beer in her mouth. *A study in borrowing patterns, the radical split between those most loaned and what makes the best-sellers lists. The press went under a month after I signed the contract,* she says, smoothing out her skirt. She smiles to herself, reads the words embedded in the tabletop. *I haven't looked at the manuscript since.*

We tried for children. Each time was harder than the last, Genevieve says, and they know enough not to ask more. But, too, they can't help remembering how avid she was years ago, when she first came to town, to head the Children's Wing.

They are quiet for a while then, sipping their drinks and clearing their throats of memory. They know what Mercedes has lost. No one needs to ask. Avis breaks their thought.

I don't know what it is I lost, she says, *but something happened after the Bronson girl. I can't put my finger on exactly what it is,* and here she runs her thumb along the edge of the table, as if to illustrate the metaphor, *but I feel it fully gone.*

Grief without an axis, Harriet says. *That's the worst kind.* They sit quietly for a few moments before they start to put on their coats.

What about me? Mercedes says.

The women look at each other tentatively, eyes drawn to the ground. *You—* Avis starts, then Harriet touches her arm, but can't keep her hand there for long. *You don't have to share,* Genevieve says, apologetically.

Mercedes looks at each of her colleagues, who do not return her gaze, and in this way, she realizes that they are scared. They're afraid she'll articulate the process and that will make them hurt, to hear what she went through. She mentioned it only once, half accidently. She is both surprised that they remembered, and not: when it is part of the body, or an idea closely linked with it—when it is part of the body that defines the body as woman, people tend to remember.

A pair of shoes, she says quietly, still seated. She takes a sip and looks out the window, where she sees it is starting to snow.

It is almost more than the librarians can take. They do their best not to look at her.

I'd been at a party in high school. It was February, but strangely warm. I remember I drank Old Fashioneds. Mercedes raises her hand to push a strand of hair from her eyes. *I walked home barefoot and the next day went back, but they were gone.*

Harriet clears her throat and Mercedes looks at her.

I know it sounds funny, but I think of them often at night.

The women sit then, reflecting on their collective pasts. No one says it, but they are all thinking the same thing: the loss women experience runs deeper than it does for men. Maybe, they all think, it is because women simply have more to lose.

When the deaf mathematician gets home, the photographer is in the basement. She walks downstairs slowly, shaking her head. When she reaches him, she hands him the envelope.

It is split cleanly across the top and he asks her, *What's this?* She pushes the envelope into his chest and smiles at the ground.

That night they have trouble opening the wine bottle. The corkscrew breaks in half.

When at last the mouth is free, they sit on the porch, she with knees to her chest and hands tucked inside her sleeves, he with one leg crossing the other so that they make an empty frame. He signs to her *I'm proud of you* and she closes her eyes and nods her head, a kind of quiet bow.

Tell me what it's about, he requests and she has to think a minute before she responds.

Rate of growth, she says, *the pattern of change over time.* She pauses and he takes a drink.

That night he teaches her how to be sure a darkroom is not breeched with light. They stand in the dark for five minutes to allow the eyes to adjust. They do not touch each other and at one point she is overcome with the feeling that he's gone. Without light to confirm it, she reaches out for proof of him somewhere in the dark but feels nothing resembling him, only the hard table, the angle of corner, the cold metal of the stop-bath rim.

For a moment he will forget himself, and her, accidentally announce the five minutes are up.

Things develop in the dark; bacteria, affection. He is grateful for it then, that what is developed is concealed, like bad shots or the poor parts of a lover, the image of his mouth moving without sound.

AN EMPTY LIBRARY IS a grave, Genevieve says at the bar. She takes a shot slowly, swallows once before it is gone and doesn't make a face when she puts the drained glass back down. *We should write a proper epitaph.*

Epigraph, Harriet says. *An empty library is as bare and kinetic as the beginning of a book.*

But we're talking about the library's death, says Genevieve.

Mercedes traces the table's script. *The beginning of a book is the end. It is the place where the author permits it sovereignty.*

And too, Avis chimes in, smearing the wet window with her hand, *an epitaph is like the title of a life, the signifier of the aftermath.*

Paper, Genevieve says, and Mercedes pulls out of her satchel a pad of paper that reads PUBLIC LIBRARY centered in all caps across the top.

The library was founded under a pseudonym, Genevieve writes.

Funded, Avis says, *the library was* funded *under a pseudonym.*

The library was founded and funded under a pseudonym, corrects Genevieve.

Therefore, Mercedes says. *Therefore…*

51

No—in effect, Avis says.

In effect, the library is said to have been discovered, Harriet says, and rises to order another round.

Genevieve looks at Mercedes, who touches Harriet's arm. She points to the far end of the table.

For the first time since the Bronson girl, they catch Avis, who is looking over the rim of her glasses at the litter of empty cups, smiling.

THE LIBRARY WAS FOUNDED AND FUNDED UNDER A PSEUDONYM. IN EFFECT, THE LIBRARY IS SAID TO HAVE BEEN DISCOVERED.

ON AVERAGE THERE ARE 57 LOVE NOTES COLLECTED FROM BETWEEN THE PAGES OF THE BOOKS PER GENRE, PER YEAR.

IT IS PERHAPS NECESSARY TO DEFINE GENRE HERE. GENRE IS DICTATED BY THE NUMBER OF CHARACTERS PRESENT IN THE TEXT.

TO CLARIFY, CHARACTERS ARE DEFINED AS ENTITIES THAT OVERTLY EXHIBIT ONE OF THE FOLLOWING PROPERTIES: INTEGRITY, AFFECTION, OR CORPORAL EXISTENCE. IT SHOULD BE NOTED THAT THESE NEED NOT BE MUTUALLY EXCLUSIVE.

ABSTRACTIONS OF CHARACTERS, OR CHARACTERS AS PRODUCTS OF FIGURATIVE LANGUAGE SUCH AS PERSONIFIED TROPES, OR WHO ARE EMBODIED BY MEANS OF METONYMIC DEVICE ARE CONSIDERED MARGINAL AND PLACED ON THE SHELVES ALONG THE INSIDE PERIMETER OF THE LIBRARY.

TO CLARIFY, A LOVE NOTE IS CHARACTERIZED AS A MISSIVE SEPARATE FROM THE ARTIFACT OF THE BOOK WITH SOME REFERENCE TO AFFECTION DECIDEDLY PRESENT.

TO CLARIFY, LOVE IS THAT WHICH IS NOT CATEGORIZED THROUGH FEELINGS OF BEING UNFOND.

I.E.:

I WANT TO EXPRESS THE DEGREE OF MY AFFECTION, BUT THE BORDERS OF THIS PAGE ARE TOO LIMINAL TO HOLD THE PROOF.

I.E.:

SOME THINGS CAN'T BE MEASURED BY THEIR OPPOSITE. FOR EXAMPLE, WHAT IS UNTHIRST? BUT WHEN YOU REALLY KNOW A THING, YOU KNOW IT UP AND DOWN. I CAN'T REMEMBER ANYMORE WHAT IT FEELS LIKE TO LEAD A LIFE UNPOLLUTED BY WHAT IS NOT THERE.

I.E.:

NOW SHE EVER-HOVERS IN THE REGION OF PERHAPS.

THE LOVE NOTES ARE COLLECTED, CATALOGED, AND BOUND. DURING THIS PROCESS, AN AVERAGE OF 14 PAPER CUTS ARE RECEIVED.

THE WINDOWS OF THE LIBRARY START TWO FEET ABOVE THE TILED GROUND AND EXTEND UP LAVISHLY SO THAT GRAND SHADOWS FALL ON THE OPEN BOOKS AND PATRONS IN THE AFTERNOONS. WEEKLY THERE CAN BE HEARD FROM ABOVE THE DULL THUD OF BIRDS HITTING WINDOWS AND FALLING IN THE CEMENT SILLS. THIS IS THE FATE OF 33 BIRDS OF 5 DIFFERENT SPECIES, ON AVERAGE, PER YEAR.

No one collects them, and after seasons of exposure to the elements the tiny bodies dissolve.

On average, 3 instances of coitus are experienced within the confines of the library annually.

An average of .5 instances of mutual arrival is experienced biannually within the library walls.

It is expected that these numbers will increase when the library is emptied. Too, it is expected that the mode of love message will shift from note to wall after the library is left bare, as there is only a certain number of days affection can be sustained and go unrecorded. On average, this number is 98.

And when the library is emptied and the building stands alone, with only its closed doors and worn carpet and the muted echo of body meeting glass, the bound collection of love notes will be emptied, too, in that way that language has when its meaning is stripped, lost, or left to settle untranslated.

Also, it should be noted that the library has no floors.

Meaning not that it lacks a foundation, but rather, that it is a structure that possesses only a single story.

THE MATHEMATICIAN COMES HOME to the photographer one night, face tear-stained and rubbed raw. She talks quickly so that her hands smear from word to word in a pattern he struggles to decipher—something about one of her students—a young one, bright—impressive midterm scores—a nasty boyfriend—the moment childhood ends—the news that the student won't become a mother after all.

The photographer opens two dark beers and pours them into tulips. He sits on the couch at a profile and she sits between his legs. He watches her hands as she talks about all kinds of things that have nothing to do with children who are not born. It is difficult to read her hands, because he is behind her, so he only gets fragments but it is more for her than him. She starts with the girl and how she is an equestrian and how a horse's gait possesses symmetry and that it reduces as the gait quickens, so that a trot is more symmetrical than a canter. She tells him there are patterns that repeat on smaller scales, a kind of reproduction, yes, but too, like the way the veins on a leaf parallel the branches of a tree and that this is what it means to say that everything expands with a memory. She talks about the beginning of zero, how it is the youngest number and what math was like before it was introduced. She tells the story of the number 4.669, why she believes it is more important than pi because it explains something significant about the way a faucet drips. She tells him that viruses are elegant, and that surplus is a curse.

At some point she asks if they have any ice cream, and he knows enough to bring the whole box.

There are people that think real death happens not when the cells of our bodies fall still, but when we are no longer remembered, she tells him and she peels off the top, buries the spoon.

But I know we each die an infinite number of times—here she breaks for another bite—*because for every decision we make, all the decisions we don't are being carried out until the future branches forward so complexly that the paths have to curve and fall around each other and the potential is endlessly dense because every singular line births thousands more and at the end of each line is a death so that we are dying always, everywhere, and what we come to know as our real death happens like a pixel on an unframed screen, so minor and forgettable, it may as well be void.*

He has to be careful here; he wants her to keep talking, because if she doesn't, he, too, will think about children who end before they begin, so he asks, *How do our beings know which trajectory to follow?*

She makes a loud snort and smiles with her spoon in her mouth, pulls it out upside down so that the curve is a cave her tongue cleans.

We follow all of them.

He reads the subtext here, that somewhere this child is not dead, that somewhere this child becomes a person and finds things important, the population paradox or the greenhouse effect, the structure of clouds or the taste of aged cheese or math or trees or photographs, maybe books or spoons, that the child either smokes or doesn't, either retires early or never gets there, owns or rents, loves a man or a woman, more than one or both, admits fault for accidents or passes them off as fate, cares about touch or doesn't, can throw a ball or knit or prove successful at crafting meals that challenge the tongue, is attractive, isn't, or exists in the space between, equates indifference to malice or affection, carries the children to bed or never has children at all. And he reads this premise of the subtext, too: that the fractured somewheres in which all of this occurs are not divorced from that which is now, here.

He stares at her hands that aren't talking, that are scraping the curved corners of the thick paper ice cream box, watches the chocolate stain her knuckles as she reaches for the bottom, watches her lick them and push her hair from her eyes, her hands pulled into her sleeves because the box is cold and he realizes there is nothing in her history that he doesn't admire—that her father had a hand in his own end, made his wife a widow before she became a mother; that she sucked her thumb long into adolescence; that when her mother learned about her daughter's hearing, she cut her own hair as close as she could to the skull; that she once stole a harmonica and still doesn't regret the way it felt on her lips; that when her students experience tragedy, they come to her, though by law they probably shouldn't, and that she cares enough to cry; that she thinks of the world as an answer to a proof and that one day this will break her heart.

She reaches the spoon backward without looking and as soon as he takes the ice cream in his mouth, she asks which of them he thinks will die first.

The ice cream thins instantly and it takes everything to keep his eyes clear, it takes everything and a full minute before he can turn her around to answer.

I don't know, but I hope it's me, he says and he feels his face shift but quickly harnesses control.

Me too, she responds and she smiles so that the question is passed off as a dark joke, but they both know they mean it. There are only two ways of managing grief: either it is overcome, or it is not.

She presses her thumb to the dip in his chin. *The ice cream has freezer burn.*

III

STUDYING DECAY

ONE DAY, WHEN THE photographer is in the basement in the dark, he hears a sound like a loud and painful wail. He flips on the light switch and runs upstairs.

When he finds her, she is in the bedroom on her knees, face to the floor looking under the bed. He pulls her to her feet and searches her body for wounds. *What is it—are you hurt?*

Yes, she says, *I lost my bookmark.*

What she calls a bookmark is the soft and tattered bit of paper with creases from folds and coffee-ring stains that reads,

The exhibit is over

He sits down on the bed, breathes out. *You scared me. I thought you were really hurt.*

She looks down at him sternly and tells him with loud hands, *I am.* She starts to pace, puts the insides of her wrists to her head.

Calm down. He sighs. *Here,* he says, grabbing the pad of paper on their bedside table, *I'll write it again.*

She rips the pad from his hands and stares into his eyes with a fury foreign to him. He knows enough to put the pen back down.

They spend the afternoon searching, under couches and between the seats of chairs, inside piles of paper, in the back of drawers. Every time he mentions it might be in a book, she snaps at him, her mouth a flat line as she speaks with loud hands—she took it out, she's sure. Keep looking.

Late that night, after she is in bed but before she falls asleep, he'll head back downstairs to resume his work. When he gets there, he sees what the light did to his shots. Ruined, he thinks, and sits in her chair, defeated. He plays with her red pen, pops the cap and snaps it back on with only his thumb until he rises from her chair, resolved.

The next morning, while he is still asleep, she walks downstairs to the kitchen to put the coffee on. There, on the kitchen table she sees a photo, a print that measures 3 x 4, smeared and stained, lesioned and scarred with light.

When he wakes up, she is sitting in bed next to him, reading. Before she leans down to kiss him, she marks her place with the print.

After work, the librarians are met with an empty bar. They remove and hang up their coats while greeting the bartender by name. He does not ask what they want, instead delivers four pints of the local brew and four whiskey shots. Then he makes his way back to the counter, where he wipes glasses out with a white cloth, raising each to the light to confirm it is clean. The women watch him, hands coiled around their mugs.

How is an e-book like a dive bar? Harriet says, watching the bartender work.

Don't use that phrase, Avis says. She studies the head on her beer. Mercedes catches Harriet's eye and nods to Avis's shaking hand.

An electronic book is not a book, Avis begins. *What makes a book is dimension. Pagination is not just splitting text in a visually consumable mass; it is recognizing a leaf of paper as a tactical entity, as an object with properties that exist in a space and evolve over passing time.* Avis uses both hands to lift her mug to her mouth. *An electronic page is mere artifice; it cannot be turned. It does not have leaves that live on two planes. It does not have a spine. Aren't these the properties of bookhood?* She searches her coworkers' eyes.

It's true, Genevieve says. *That we say a story "unfolds" is not insignificant here. Our conception of literature is rooted in the physical act of reading. As the weight of the pages in the left hand increases, so does our emotional preparation for reveal. I mean, really, what is more captivating than being inside a half-finished book? What is more mesmeric than sensing that collection of matter slimming in the crease of the right palm?*

Avis pushes her index finger into the tabletop for emphasis. *A story is not displayed. A story is opened. We do not witness stories; we enter them.*

Genevieve leans back from the table. *An electronic book is just a mechanical photo album,* she says. *It's the collected pictures of the pages of a manuscript on a warm and glowing device. It isn't a book at all.*

Harriet audibly huffs, shakes her head. *Listen to yourselves,* she says, looking out the window. She cannot tell if what falls is rain or snow. *The meaning of book is changing. You have to learn to shift.*

There are some things that should not change, Avis says. She holds up her shot of whiskey. *There are some things,* she nods to her shot glass, *that should be left alone. The things we find richest—those are the things we do not let anyone change.*

You're wrong, Harriet says. She takes the shot glass from the air and puts it to her lips. *If you really love a thing, you change with it. That is how you do not let it die.* Harriet tips the glass into her mouth.

All the women look at the table. Mercedes breaks their thought. *But in order for the library to die, mustn't it first be living?*

That night the women prepare to leave in silence, wrapping sheer scarves around their heads and pulling gray gloves over their achy hands, holding their pocketbooks tightly to their breasts before they exit the doors.

Excuse me? a voice says, and the women turn around to see the bartender standing behind them, face flushed and glossy with sweat, using his apron to dry his hands.

I've got it, he says and the women are silent, staring. They notice that the sweat stains from under his arms almost to his chest. *How an e-book is like a dive bar*, he says.

The women look at Mercedes, who looks at the ground. The bartender walks past them and tugs on the beaded metal string hanging from the neon OPEN sign. The entranceway becomes suddenly dim. The women smell stale beer and soap over a hint of masculine musk. It brings them each back to their youth in private ways. He holds the door open for them and they move, single file onto the street. He smears the sweat from his forehead with the back of his hairy hand and looks at them with wide blue eyes.

No cover, the bartender says.

That night, each woman spends time in front of the books in her home, correcting those that have been dog-eared. Each has a nightcap, toasts alone to the technologies that become extinct along with the page; verso and recto, the notion of weight, hardcover and bookmark.

That night, each of the women toasts to the practices that cease along with the book, the touch of finger to tongue before one turns the page.

SOME MORNINGS THEY WAKE at dawn for walks. They layer their clothes in the dark of their room with the blinds drawn. In silence they pour strong coffee into dark mugs and zip each other up. Outside, the frost covers everything that doesn't move, the residue of night. By the time they return it will be gone.

When she was young she used to think of the power of weather. She would read about the adolescents that crashed their cars on local roads or the elderly who fell on sidewalks, the children who went into the pond because of ice. Once she read about a man impaled with a falling icicle. How strange, she thought then, a mug in her hand, her mother in the other room ironing, her father not yet gone, that winter leaves us hurt in ways that do not exist in other months. How strange, she thought, bringing the mug to her lips, that the source of death—the cold—with time is gone.

On the walks she takes with the photographer, they do not speak. They walk slowly and think about what they see, a practice that began as vocabulary lessons when he'd started to sign. It is only later, after their day is done, that they will articulate what they observed; the empty cartridge of a firework, the mauled corpse of a mole, the fresh paint dividing the road, a bottle cap from a rare brand of beer, a large moth with only one wing, a pencil boasting the name of the library, the freshly cut grass in front of the abandoned house, a plastic flower barrette, a single shoe standing up and without lace.

For a few months when they first started, the photographer was careful not to mention sounds. She noticed this right away and almost objected, but now it takes no effort for him not to mention them.

They are almost to the point at which they turn around when he reaches for her arm.

You know, he says, *if your theory of fractured future is right, in some worlds we haven't met.*

Later, she will think she almost made it up, what she thought she saw hidden in the ditch. The water must have played a trick on her, she will think, the way it can with reflection or bending objects that are straight. In subsequent weeks she will strive for a glimpse of it again, linger in the place she swore it surfaced in her memory, leave unsatisfied, confused.

She realizes he is right, that in some worlds they haven't met, and looks at the ditch with a foot of water to see a drowned book. It is closed and she cannot make out the title, but it haunts her the way a loose limb might and she looks away.

She takes off her mitten and grabs his hand, answers him only with touch. She can feel the raised scars on his palms.

She feels him waiting for her response, but this passes after just a few strides.

She knows that in worlds they haven't met, and in others they have, but things are different—he learns to leave the bed unmade, preserving the casts of their forms, and she learns to make it, to wipe the slate clean, start fresh with ordered sheets.

She knows in worlds they haven't met but she thinks then that he chooses not to articulate the obviously sadder potential: that in some worlds they never will.

THIS IS HOW THE photographer knows that love is the study of change: it is first ice cubes melting along the thin muscle on the inside of her thigh, her damp toothbrush, the rush of risk. And afterward, the wet smell of flowers, revised plans, paying off her debt.

Come nights, the photographer pours himself wine in mugs and watches the videos he took of her. He had compromised, refused to photograph her, but since she wanted documentation, proof, he taped them now and then. Now he watches the films for hours, featuring nothing in particular, her shifting back and forth across the kitchen counter doing dishes, shaving her legs in the tub, sleeping at night, the rise and fall of her chest like an inverted metronome.

Sometimes, in bed, she took out a tape measure and wrapped him in it, recording her results. He watched her move around him: she the scientist, he the subject, the study. She kept her notes in her bedside table drawer and periodically adjusted them: the loss of a fraction of an inch around the thigh, a gain at the waist. One night she asked if he wanted to try, and when he said *Why?* her answer came through hands so matter-of-fact that he was ashamed to have asked.

Dimension, she said, her forehead crimped, the tape measure set between her teeth. *Practicing good love is knowing their body better than your own,* she said, and pulled the pencil from her hair, made a quick mark in her notebook, and stretched him out on the bed.

Now he sits watching her on the screen, sleeping, her mouth slightly open, the features of her face comfortable, relaxed.

He is surprised when suddenly his thumb breaches the camera's frame. He had almost forgotten he'd been on the other side.

THE EDIFICE IS A bathtub, a darkroom, a mouth. The edifice is the blood at the cleave of her legs, the way it smells like coins. This is the mechanism, she thinks, that structures both the go and the come.

She has to remind herself how to eat again, to relearn that taste takes time. She has to learn to let food sit on her tongue before she swallows. It is like learning to walk, or talk with hands. It is like learning that air is an entity, more than idea: that there are elements we cannot sense that are always at work. The force that allows an ice cube to melt, she thinks, filling the ladle with soup. The force that determines that space between seeing the breath and not.

A spoon enters a mouth, the lips wrap its pit and move the broth bath. Afterward, she will wash and dry it, set the spoons one on top of another so they sit fixed, stacked together in organized files. A column of spoons is something to admire, the way they arch in unison. A heap of ordered spoons is something to care about, she thinks, and fingers the cove on the top of the pile.

An empty library sits in the middle of its grounds as futile and passive as the tongue at rest in the hollow of the mouth.

Since the library is now closed on Saturdays, the librarians stay out late Friday nights. At two in the morning the women are still going strong.

You know, Genevieve says, *just because the library will close doesn't mean the world will stop reading.*

Avis yawns and covers her mouth. *You're right. Reading is private; a relationship between the self and the text.*

Harriet rolls an empty shot glass between her flat palms. The women listen to the ting of her wedding ring hitting the thick glass. *But there has to be discourse, right? It can't simply be consuming in a void.*

The discourse happens between the book and the reader, Avis tells them, rolling her head on her neck.

They hear the faint voice of the bartender telling them it's last call.

Reading has to be a public act. If only the text and the reader participate in the exchange, then how does knowledge get used?

But you don't read to talk about what you've read. You read to let thought loiter in the mind. Genevieve finishes her drink. *You read to be alone.*

Maybe, Avis says. *Okay, maybe. But if it is a private act, then why endorse a space for communal reading? If it is a private act, then what are libraries for?*

Economics, Harriet says. *Access. Temporally speaking, the library book is simply more often in use.* Harriet puts the shot glass down and places both palms on the table.

They think then about next Monday, how after the doors are locked tightly they'll gather books to put in their trunks. At home, their collections are growing, and they're happy to shelve them without regard to structure or organized plan. They let them float unclassified, so that the covers of strange books touch each other; authors with last names on opposite ends of the alphabet, genres that sat on converse walls inside the library's stacks. After years of enforcing order, they like to think they've let the books free.

Avis tips her glass so she can see her reflection and talks to it with wide eyes when she says, *They want to re-term our positions.*

All the women look at her. They hear the bartender repeat that it's last call.

They want to retire the term "librarian."

Mercedes shakes her head. *I don't understand. What else could we possibly be called?*

Avis glances up at the ceiling and sighs. *Information science technicians.*

They each make a noise like the sound of giving up. Harriet orders their last round.

But book care isn't a science, it's an art, Mercedes says, her face pinched with concern.

The three other women stare at her then, study the look in her eyes.

The drinks come and they start to pass them out, nod gently to the bartender and watch him walk away. The bartender turns off the neon OPEN sign and tells a man walking in it's last call.

74

Harriet, Avis, and Genevieve are silent then, watching their colleague trace the words carved into the tabletop. The bartender reminds them of Mercedes informing the patrons of close.

They all think the same thing: that the end will be hardest for her.

IN THE DARKROOM, SHE watches him work. Today he is aiming for transposed shots, working with only the negatives to make new prints. They move her chair next to the light switch and they hold the two ends of a string. She spends the afternoon there, managing the dark.

She watches him work, her head at a tilt, studies the faces he makes. They run the gamut of emotions: surprise, concern, satisfaction, suspicion, malaise.

Light, he signs to her and she flips the switch off.

In the dark she's alone with her thoughts. She recalls vaguely a conversation they'd had some months back, when she asked him the thesis of photography.

To make experience stand still, he told her and refilled her coffee mug.

I know. But why? To prove? To provide evidence? Or to distort?

I think that would depend on the photographer, he said. And then, *I like to think I prove. Sort of just like you.*

There is a tug on the string she holds in her hand and she turns the light back on. When she does, she feels a hint of pain behind her eyes as they adjust to the light.

She tugs the string back and he looks up, confused. Apparently, she thinks, he's told himself this only works one way.

How does transposing two shots provide evidence of the world? she asks. It takes him a minute to understand what she's asking, and when he does he looks back down at his work. She tugs again, and when he looks up she says, *Well?*

How do you know that the photos I'm making now aren't happening somewhere else? he signs back and returns his gaze to his work.

Before she has time to respond, he signs to her, *light,* and she flips the switch off. Later, when she looks at the photos, she will understand what he means; they still purport reality, only not the past.

She is quick as she works her arms out of her sleeves, careful to be as quiet as she can. She knows that words don't always work when it comes to proof.

When the tug comes and the light returns, she is standing next to the door, all her clothes at her feet.

In an empty library someone has scribed on the wall in spray paint, *Where do you go when you come?*

On the porch one morning, the photographer hands the deaf mathematician the newspaper. He refills her coffee mug and watches her as she reads.

On page two, the deaf mathematician learns that the library catalog can now be accessed online, thus allowing local patrons access to nearly twenty times more texts.

That's so sad, she says after handing it back.

Sad? He asks her.

She nods. *I don't want anything to change. I want it all to stay exactly like it is.*

The photographer laughs, shaking his head. *That's not a terribly healthy way to live, especially today. ESPECIALLY,* he says, spelling out each letter of the word, *for a scientist. You stick to that thinking and you'll drive yourself straight toward insane.*

It's simple to stay sane—you just forget, she tells him. She tops off his mug. *Take this, for example. Every year these doctors from the university come into our school and try to recruit the faculty and staff to participate in testing for cochlear implants. They do this every year. And for one day we let it get under our skin. And then we just forget. Until, of course, that one day the next year when they come back.*

They both break here for a sip, and he thinks for a moment that she's never told him this. Then he lets himself think briefly of what it would be like to hear her voice.

And what do you tell them? he asks, burying his thought.

She looks out at the front yard for a moment before she responds. *I'm quiet. I listen and nod and then watch them walk away, every year alone, with no recruits.* She rests her head on the back of the chair and turns her neck in order to smile at him.

You know, he says, *you can only stay neutral for a while, before serious advance takes place.* Her smile fades and she buries her mouth in her mug. She pulls her legs to her chest, her bare feet pointing down over the edge of the chair. *There are going to be debates soon about the end of deafness—"fixed" children "corrected" in the womb. You are going to have to think about where you stand.*

She takes a minute before she responds. *Where I stand is scared,* she says and lets out a deep sigh. *But not for us. Not for us,* she says.

For a minute he thinks the "us" means she and him, but then it's clear who she is talking about.

If that's "advance" I'd worry, she says. She takes another sip. *Because it means we've abandoned formal logic.* She looks at him with the smallest sliver of a grin. *Don't they know a post-deaf world means not knowing what it is to hear?*

ONE DAY WHEN THE photographer takes a day trip to pick up a collection of whisks for his next project, the deaf mathematician finds herself standing in front of the library in the rain. This morning she had awoken alone. As she sat in bed looking up at the cracks in the ceiling, she realized this had not happened in months, her waking in bed without him. She was almost disappointed not to have the debate about whether or not to make the bed.

She needed to be close to him then, so she trekked to the library, hoping to look at his work.

It was not raining when she left, but by the time she makes it to the front entrance it is coming down in sheets. And when she pulls the entrance doors, she is surprised to be locked out. She cups her hands around her eyes to look inside, where she sees low lights and a lone librarian, the one who is always angry, sitting at the counter with a book.

The deaf mathematician knocks on the door and Avis looks up, waves her hand away. The deaf mathematician steps back from the doors to catch a sign on light blue construction paper. In calligraphy, someone has written:

Library hours have been reduced.

Saturday–Sunday: closed

The deaf mathematician knocks again and Avis pulls her feet down from the counter, walks over to the door.

The deaf mathematician points to the restroom and Avis, recognizing the woman, lets her in.

In the bathroom, the deaf mathematician sits on the closed toilet lid, thinking of what it means to have a library that's empty inside. If a library is anything, it is a place that is full, of patrons or books, of ideas and what she assumes would be silence. The deaf mathematician sneezes into her sleeve and reads the graffiti on the wall of the bathroom stall. She thinks about where these walls will go if the building is put to rest or collapsed, like the set from a stage. Is the library the building or the books? she thinks. It is an edifice as certain but abstract as math.

When she leaves the bathroom she walks up to Avis, whose eyes are scanning a book. She is feeling something akin to sympathy, or maybe just regret. The deaf mathematician wants to tell the librarian that she knows about end and what it means to reach it, that studying growth means studying decay.

The deaf mathematician touches Avis's hand and Avis looks at what is happening on the desk as though her hand were divorced from the rest of her body. The deaf mathematician strokes the thin skin on the top of her hand, then pats it gently three times. Avis watches the scene as though it were something grotesque she might stare at on the street and then realize with shame she was looking and quickly turn away.

The deaf mathematician pulls out her notebook and begins to write. Avis looks at her then, the way her part sits, slants across her forehead, the way her bag strap cuts across her chest; she is all angle, Avis thinks. And then, no wonder the photographer sees something here.

The deaf mathematician tears off the sheet of paper and folds it once, slides it across the desk. She walks out the door and wraps her arms around her center, defending against the cold. Avis watches her look both ways at the crosswalk. Avis watches until she reaches the other side. She thinks of the Bronson girl then; her own wide grin as she stamped the book, turned it around to face the girl and slid it to where her body reached the counter, at the chin. How the girl took it and said *thank you very much* and walked out the doors, her gait so quick and full of spring Avis thought she might trip. How when Avis thought this she laughed to herself. How it was raining, and she watched the girl put up the hood of her slicker, look to the left, the only direction she should have needed to look. How the librarians had wanted to change the one-way road out front because of traffic build-ups on weekends, had taken their case to the county and lost. How the girl had started with that gait across the walk and never reached the other side. How Avis had not been the same—woman or librarian, person or friend. How she had been changed in ways she thought were impossible at her age, after all she'd already lost. How it was the sound that bothered her most, the sound of the child's body hitting the car and the way the girl did not scream, was fully and totally mute and the way the echo of that noise haunts her sometimes at arbitrary moments: in the shower, or in line at the grocery store; as she's making the bed, or when she's getting the mail. And how, for a reason she cannot determine the source of, she will think of the deaf women who is loved by the photographer then, how fortunate it is that she cannot hear.

Avis looks down at the note sitting on the desk. She can almost make out the sound of Mercedes's voice saying, *Please make your choices and make your way up front.* They are turning into ghosts.

She unfolds the paper.

It is a mathematical certainty that there exists a world
in which the library will never close

it reads. And for the first time ever, though she is ashamed and holding back emotion she has always been sure to control, Avis allows herself to think, if only for a moment, that maybe it's better that the library end.

IV

THE REST IS ALL REFRACTION

THE DEAF MATHEMATICIAN IS in the tub shaving. The photographer sits on the closed toilet lid smoking and reading the news.

She glances at his face, which she reads as confused. She snaps her fingers and he looks up and then she signs, *What?*

The library is implementing DVD rental, he tells her, and she sets the razor down on the spout, bends her legs so her knees rise above the water's crest.

Sorites paradox, she signs to him and pulls the chain cord connected to the tub's rubber plug. He hears the thunder of water emptying but she doesn't move and they watch the tiny spiral develop at the mouth of the drain. He studies it instead of asking her to explain.

Weeks later he will look it up.

When do grains become a pile? he reads.

He sits down at the kitchen table. When does aching become pain?

When does a building that holds books lose the status of being a library?

A LIBRARY MIGHT ONLY be deemed such if there are books inside. What, then, is the function of the building that stands bookless, other than to amplify the echo of dead birds collecting on the windowsills?

It is the night before the first day of another year. The photographer and the mathematician are sitting in the dark of the living room, eyes wide with the blue hue of the television screen. They are watching a silent film.

When they are like this, sometimes the photographer thinks of what it would be like if she could hear. He imagines the things she misses: the click of the camera's shutter or the chirping of the turn signal, the dull ping of hail on wet wood. Sometimes he imagines making a wind chime of her spoons so that she could know them other than through touch.

He picks up the remote control and turns the volume up. He listens to the nothing recorded there, the sheer drone of silence, and looks into his glass. He can feel the alcohol working through his arms and legs, his hands. It feels good to him, the way it feels when he has trouble falling asleep and she runs her fingers over his scalp. It feels good, like when she put her hands over his to teach him signs, how she would shape his fingers, extend and contract his arms, lift his eyebrows or push down the ends of his lips. It aroused him in a very lethargic way. But now the tutoring is done. He knows the language well enough not to need her aide. Sometimes he looks up complex mathematical terms and asks her to help him pronounce, just to feel her managing his hands, to feel her making his body talk to both of them.

When the photographer looks up from his glass he sees her face in the low light, her head resting on a pillow, her eyes drawn shut. Her legs are folded to make room for him on the couch, and when he pulls her legs across his lap, she stirs. *Cold*, she signs, and he rises to adjust the heater. He does not smell the heat. He rests his head so that he looks at her. The screen goes unwatched.

Somewhere they are turning things together: a steering wheel, a waterspout, the handle of a door. Time is less a dial than a screw; it turns and returns, but also simultaneously descends.

COME NIGHTS, THE PHOTOGRAPHER disbands his prints to re-suture them. He takes photographs of what were set events, sears them and reorders so that they tell the stories that did not happen.

She has asked him to put one in the bathroom, so that she might look at it while she's in the tub. She is in the tub now, watching him hold the frame to the wall, move it up and down. She shifts and he hears the water's movement. Finally she makes a quiet *hmm* and he looks back to see her nodding, signing *Right there.* The pencil he has held behind his ear is used to make a tiny mark. The nail he has held in his mouth is pushed into the wall.

When it is hung, he sits on the closed toilet lid, reaches for his cigarettes. She begins to lather her legs, ready to put the razor to her skin, but she pauses to look up at the photo. She starts when she sees what it holds, crimps the skin above her eyes. It is the drowned book she saw on one of their walks, the book she thought had developed in her mind since she'd never found it again.

She makes a loud splash in the water with her hand and he looks. *You saw it?* she asks, and when he looks confused, she points at the photograph. He doesn't respond.

The book. The book in the water, on the last leg of our walks. A year or so ago. The book in the water in the ditch, she tells him, and he looks at the photo hard.

He sets down the newspaper in order to speak. *This is transposed,* he tells her slowly, *two images I cohered. You saw this?* he asks.

For a moment possibility hovers in the tiny room, divorces itself from the water's steam, his cigarette smoke, so that it is almost visible.

No, she signs back tersely. *I must have made it up.*

She starts to work on her legs and he listens to the soft sound of brisk scrape, watches the way her head nods just a bit, at an angle, the way her arm works from ankle to the thickest part of her thigh, which peeks out from the skin of sudsy water, her eyes following the blade. He would give it all up to be that long draw, spend the rest of his life in a world where she only shaved her legs.

I will need you exactly always, the photographer tells her then.

She looks at him and her eyes are soft but strangely wide. She slips her leg into the water, dissolving her lather. She reaches out her hand and dries it on the tail of his shirt. Then she takes the cigarette from his mouth. When she inhales, she closes her eyes.

At the library, a bird hits the window and falls to the ground. But within the same moment it moves, and shortly after flies away.

ONE MORNING, BEFORE THEY unlock the doors, the librarians gather in one of the silent rooms. They sit Genevieve down at the tiny table. The rest of them stand.

We need to talk, Avis tells her. Genevieve looks up at them, confused.

We've done an informal survey, Harriet says, *and it seems that the patrons want some changes in the Children's Wing.*

Genevieve shakes her head. *I don't understand.*

The animals on the walls are too childish, Avis says.

But it's the CHILDREN'S Wing.

They want sleek, modern, Harriet says. *And it's not the Children's Wing anymore. It's the Space for Pre-Adults.*

But aren't Pre-Adults children? Genevieve asks, looking up at each of them.

Not anymore, Mercedes tells the floor.

WE ARRIVE THROUGH TOUCH; a fist knocks on a door. Then there is the aftermath, the acts of eating and sleeping, the moving about, the finding things important. The end is entering that door and coming to understand that in entering, the house is empty.

She taught him to lose his voice like a skin. And his hearing, too; this was more a task than a decision. Now, standing in the kitchen, he has started to talk to himself, considering aloud what to do with her shoes and her books, the marker he used to write on her skin.

For weeks he had thought he was imagining the buzzing he heard throughout the house. It is when he reaches for the bourbon that he realizes it is not a product of his mind; when he opens the cabinet it grows louder and ends when he touches the shelf. It is the champagne flutes, their thin glass skin holding nothing, two adjacent slight curves touching, the contact inducing the sound. He lifts his hand from the shelf and the hum is reignited and when he uses his index finger to split the tangent, there is no greater gaping than that liminal space between the glasses, divorcing the singular world of what is from the infinite realms of what isn't.

And he is filled with wonder, thinking of all the places she is not, thinking that she is ultimately now nowhere, and asking, as he pulls the bourbon from the shelf, glancing at the negatives on the refrigerator door, what is the something making the glasses move?

How he knows there is something to learn from lack, from loss: he has studied the vacant veins of her lipstick-stained glasses, the routes where the chapped skin did not touch the glass. He knows the webs of clear between her bulky blots. There is something to say for echo, for image; the marks survive, though the lips are gone.

A POSED QUESTION REQUIRES response. What, then, does it mean that she has started asking questions to the walls of the shower, the water scalding her skin until it is blemished, one hand on the curtain's bar to keep her steady, the other on her hip, head down so she can see how quickly everything drains, speaking to no one but herself?

This winter was another one. He never cared much for the season, and when in the middle of the night she wakes to lightning outside, she seats herself in the kitchen to watch it blinking behind the falling snow. An anomaly, she thinks, sipping her champagne. If proof were reached through sight, how different our world would be.

When she was young she was told to watch her mouth or her mouth would be washed clean. The taste of soap thick on her lips, the deaf mathematician would fall into fitful sleep. If asked, she would say that being in bed alone is the hardest part; after his death there is no one to hold her like a spoon, stroke the skin beneath her shirt, finger the pocket of her navel, that universal scar. When asked, she would call it a haunting, the taste of soap, reminding her each night to always keep an eye on her tongue.

And where were the hands in all of this? she thinks now, watching the snow, wondering if the thunder can be heard. She gets her answer when she sets down her glass, feels the shudder passing from the structure of her floors into the wood of the table and up through her arms. How we mix our metaphors, she thinks, shaking her head at her flute. How sad we are, always striving to reduce.

THE DEAF MATHEMATICIAN IS in the tub shaving. She has her foot on the top of the water spout and is drawing the razor the full length of her leg, from the ankle to mid-thigh. He is sitting on the closed toilet lid, reading the newspaper. He puts it down and reaches over to the tub, where he puts three fingers in and moves them back and forth to get her attention.

Look at this, he tells her and holds up the front page. The photographer offers one side of his unbuttoned flannel shirt and she dries her hands before she takes the paper.

There is a photo of a couple on either side of a ditch that runs haphazardly through a neatly trimmed cornfield: the man is standing to the far left of the shot in the distance a bit and at a profile, looking toward where the frame ends. His hands are in his pockets. The woman is the fore figure, kneeling on the ground and facing straight ahead. Her hands are wrapping her sweater tighter around her body and her face is caught mid-sob. Her loose hair is pulled to the right, away from the man, by the wind. The eye is drawn last to the gaping sky, which composes most of the shot and is poignantly cloudless.

He watches her read the single line of text that runs underneath. *Don't you think that's wrong?* he asks her. *Their children's bodies are right there in that ditch.* He points to the center of the frame.

She thinks for a while, and he sees her eyes scan the whole picture, twice, three times. She hands the paper back.

You would never know that without reading the caption, she tells him. *I think it's moving.*

He stares at her and she makes a few more strokes of the razor before she returns his gaze.

He isn't sure why, but he thinks of the library then. He thinks about loss and how to quantify it, how we have a tendency to reduce all loss to the same sum in the end. He has heard similar theories about the way the mind cannot comprehend tragedy in numbers greater than twelve, so that a plague becomes equivalent to a single-car accident. He tries to imagine how many books are in the library, how they'll disperse in a way that erases their history after the building is closed.

But we did read the caption. We know the bodies of their twins are just yards behind them, he insists. *Don't you find that cruel?*

The deaf mathematician pulls her foot from the top of the water spout and turns toward him.

We can't see anything. We can't see the bodies.

He shakes his head from left to right. He tells her that the knowledge is more haunting than the image, that it is because we can't see the bodies that it fails in principle. *If the bodies were in the shot, the photo would never have been printed,* he says.

Wrong, she says. *They would have been carefully cut out.*

They sit silently for a minute and he wants to ask her something important about math but doesn't.

You don't think this is a breach of ethics?

The deaf mathematician lathers her leg. She dips her hands in the water before she speaks, and when she does she wields her hands gently but resolved, so that her tone is tender but the spray of bath water is felt on his face.

For whom? Maybe the parents, but they recognize this photo is no relic. It's only in the paper for a day; that is what designates document from art. And certainly not the photographer—it's her function to capture the world as accurately and fully as possible, not excluding what is ugly or painful or cruel. And above all not the children; they are dead. The deaf mathematician reaches out her hand to touch her lover's arm. Then she goes on to say she thinks it's a beautiful photograph. *Don't you know that in order for art to work, you've got to suspend your disbelief? You have to forget a man with a camera stood in front of them as they learned the news. You have to forget that he probably took more than one shot and that he gets paid to chronicle the tragic, to satiate our demand for the sad.*

The photographer raises his hands to respond and she grabs them midair, pushes them into the silence that sits in this lap.

In order for life to work, you've got to suspend your disbelief. You've got to forget that everything ends, she says.

He looks at the photo of the drowned book in the frame in front of him. *Or,* he tells her, *you have to believe that it doesn't.*

They stare at each other and then at the photo in the newspaper. She takes in a deep breath and sighs hard as she asks, *Don't you think it is beautiful?*

But he looks away before he catches her question, so she only asks the air. All he can think is that this is why he can never photograph people. Broken wine glasses and rusted spoons can be moving without forfeiting moral law. He hears her pull the plug and looks over, notices the goose bumps on her skin.

Anyway, she tells him, her eyes flat. *Math is just a language.* She stands and he has to look up to watch her talk. *At least you love something you can touch.*

AFTER THE DOORS ARE locked, the librarians place books into boxes to carry to their cars. They take the books in box loads now to make room for the wide tables that will fill the far west wall. When the women tell Mercedes, she doesn't understand. *So the patrons have room to work on their computers,* Harriet tells her, and then, when she still looks confused, *because the stacks are no longer required for browse.*

The bar is full tonight, but they see from outside as they approach that their table is clear. When they walk in, fighting the line at the door, they notice a tiny marker on their table informing them that the seats are reserved. Avis looks at the bartender, busy taking orders, but he notices her and locks eyes, nods. She nods back and tells her colleagues to sit down.

After three rounds they are silent for a while in that way that too much drink too quickly can make a small group. They each reflect on the coming end.

What I'm concerned with most, Harriet tells them, leaning in close, *is that the access to everything will lead to the possession of noth-*

ing at all. They seem to forget that the job of a librarian is not just acquisition—it is stripping the library clean of the bad books, too.

That's an archaic logic now, Genevieve says, staring blankly at the graffiti on the tabletop. *That's the antithesis of the whole new wave; not that everything is art, but that we each have the power to decide what isn't. That's what uncensored access is. The antidote to privilege.*

Maybe our theories are simply growing too old, Mercedes says, fingering the rim of her mug.

No, Avis says. *I can't believe that.*

But it's true. A library is by nature an inherently censored space. And we're the ones keeping books out.

The library has at its center a clearly conflicted premise, Harriet says. *We fancy ourselves making the word freely heard but we don't because we can't. We're restricted by the frame of the building itself. The web is the answer and I'm not so sure it's wrong. It reminds me of that old riddle. What came first, humans or language?*

It's language that got us into this mess, Genevieve says, finishing her drink.

Isn't it humans? Mercedes responds.

Everyone looks at the table, not reading the words inscribed there.

She means text, Avis says.

No, Genevieve starts, *what I mean is terms. What I mean is, what does the word "library" denote anymore? It used to mean a building that holds books. The idea of collected texts. A public space endorsing the communal act of reading. But it's none of those anymore.*

The women are quiet, thinking. All of their glasses stand half empty of beer.

Over half the catalog currently sits in our four separate homes. What does that make the place we report to each day? And if we can't answer that, then what are we? She picks up her glass to take another sip but at the last moment pulls it from her lips to say, *Don't you see we're becoming obsolete?*

Yes, Harriet says. *Yes, I do. But I'm not sure our jobs are the focus anymore. Isn't it the library we should be saving?*

Sure. And that's just what we're trying to do, Genevieve says. She looks each of them in the eyes before she speaks again. *I just can't help thinking, in bed, at night, that all we are saving are books.*

The women breathe deeply and do not speak. From outside the bar, their table stands framed in window. Everything inside and behind them moves; people talking, laughing, ordering another round. But the women at the table are still, heads hung and hands in their laps.

Then Mercedes speaks. Her voice is quiet and they all lean in to hear her.

Sometimes at night, as I'm falling asleep, during the time when my father used to read me bedtime stories, I think of all the copies of one singular story out there in the world. How that book is being read hundreds, millions of times, over and over again. How multitudes of people are reading it simultaneously. And in my head, this lets me believe that the book will never really end, because it is always being begun somewhere again—and it is never the same. It is always a different story, as different from one person to the next as it is for you now compared to when you were a child. Mercedes absently fingers the words on the tabletop and the others put down their beers. *You enter a book knowing it will end. You read toward that end hoping to forget it is there. You flip each page, recognize you're getting closer, but you still hope something will change, that somehow the story will live on, past the cover's close.* Mercedes pauses for a sip from her mug, swallows and clears her throat. *That is what a library does. It is the structure that lets these stories live out and pass on. It provides the scaffolding for this to happen in one singular, specified space. The book is the story's body, the channel through which events and characters live circuitously, through repetition, through circulation, and the library is the place that sustains that act, that endorses the now-primitive rules of borrow and share.* She finishes the beer left in her mug and sets it back down on the table, pushes it away from her chest. *It is The Library where we come together to defend against the end. Not some abstract, intangible web we cannot touch.*

When Mercedes looks up at her colleagues they are nodding, lips pursed and turned down slightly at the edge. Their eyes are glossy, she notices, and their lips are chapped.

Every night they drink, Avis thinks as the bartender asks if they want another round, but every morning they are thirsty again.

DESCRIBE TO ME ECHO, she asks. It is morning and they are in bed, falling in and out of sleep. He sits up and lights a cigarette, looks up at the wall and studies the water stains there. They are wide and getting wider as the seasons pass. The mold could be poisoning the air, he thinks. He takes another long drag and decides to take care of it soon.

Echo, she asks. What is it?

He would never tell her but at night he has started to dream of her voice. It comes after he asks her a question and it is devastating, the way the news of sudden death busts logic. She told him once that there is an equation in which $1 = 0$ and when he has the dream, her voice strikes him like it did that day, when she executed and explained the proof. He remembers the knowledge settling in, a haunting. First everything seems so fully absolute. And then, with one word or number, something he knows as fact is quickly and cleanly undone. He cannot help thinking that everything we know must possess this property. He is careful to stop before hypothesizing about the source of the force keeping sense tightly intact.

Echo, he tells her after ashing his cigarette, *is like a photo in which the frame is always made smaller through crop until there is nothing left.*

She sits up in the bed and smoothes out the sheets, folds them neatly over her chest. *Everyone always describes it like a wave, like a great bubble that gets bigger until it climaxes and falls.*

He glances behind her at the cast of her head left in the pillowcase. *No,* he says, *that's just because we think of sound as smallest when it exits the mouth. But really, it is loudest then. The rest is all refraction, like the light from a prism, only channeled.*

She looks at him for a long time after he rests his hands. Then she looks out the window at the slowly falling snow. Her view is invaded by his wave. She turns to watch him speak.

Describe to me silence, he asks.

She pulls the cigarette out of his mouth and helps herself to a drag before grinding it into the tray. Then she says, *I don't know what that is.*

Look here, Mrs. Bronson tells her husband. She shows him the newspaper.

Faulty heater, she says as her husband scans the page. She dries her hand with the dishtowel and puts her wedding ring back on.

Says here the woman was deaf, Mr. Bronson tells his wife.

Mrs. Bronson looks out the window at the empty swing that hangs stationary in their backyard, keeps her eyes there when she says, *Which would be worse? To be left to die that way or to be the one that remains alone?*

Her husband looks at her. He watches her pull the wedding ring from the base of her finger up and over her knuckle and then push it back down, follows her gaze toward the backyard. When his stare meets the swing set he looks back at the newspaper.

That poor woman, Mr. Bronson says.

No, his wife tells him, closing the window shade, making her way over to the table to refill his coffee cup, *that poor man.*

WHEN A TRAJECTORY SPLITS, it is not a daunting task. It is equivalent in force to the pivot of a foot. It is as simple and quiet as the branching of a tree, the veins under our skin. It happens as silently and painlessly as making up your mind.

The deaf mathematician and the photographer sleep in the morning that possibility splits. They set the alarm for eleven and don't move before it goes off. There is something about the winter and the warmth of each other's bodies, the touch of flesh and sleep. Later, they will remember this, think of the force that kept them in bed, how if the events of that morning had to be reduced to one variable, it would be cold.

While the deaf mathematician and the photographer are upstairs, holding each other in bed, a book sits on the kitchen table. It is a small volume, clothbound and dog-eared, the title of which is embossed. The spine is broken, writing riddles the margins, and inside the small envelope in the inside cover, a library card has been placed. The book contains a two-page epilogue.

Too, the due date for the book is today.

Upstairs the alarm clock sounds.

GENEVIEVE IS LOCKING THE doors when her pencil slips from her bun. When she reaches down to pick it up, she notices a small and tattered sheet of paper lying on the floor, wedged in the front desk's recess near the floor. She slides it out from under the desk with her foot. She does not know that it is the photographer's handwriting. She reads it and her eyes gloss a bit, and she holds it to her chest and looks up, blinks quickly for a minute or two.

When she hears Harriet call her name, she does not notice how long the echo lives.

IF THE BOOK IS not returned, the deaf mathematician and the photographer will be fined.

If the photographer returns the book, then the deaf mathematician will ascend the stairs. She will draw a bath. She'll put her hand under the running water, feel the thunder from the spout. She will look at the photo he framed and placed on the wall near the mirror. She will slowly undress and she will shut tightly the door.

If the deaf mathematician returns the book, then the photographer will descend the stairs. He'll enter his darkroom to develop last week's work. He will glance at the red pen sitting in her corner chair. Then he'll bolt the door shut and flip the switch off, wait in the dark for the light.

But if both the deaf mathematician and the photographer return the book, and if they do not do so together but in separate realms, then possibility, which until this point has been a gaping void, is both realized and splits.

As they each step out the front door, the single book doubles to two, the volume held tightly in each of the lovers' arms, they do not know it is their final parting, nor that it happens twice. That this knowledge escapes them is part of what keeps us moving from day to day; we know death is coming, but we pretend it is not. This is the thesis of being: we drive forth in order to reach the end, yet doing so is our protection against remembering that it is there.

In other words, we repeat the same behavior hoping for different results.

THE DEAF MATHEMATICIAN AND the photographer have only coffee for breakfast. They spend the morning looking out the window, at the way their tree is covered in ice thick enough to catch the falling snow. They watch the limbs grow low with the weather's accumulation and they do not speak.

The book sits on the corner of the kitchen table. Aside from it and the coffee mugs, the table is bare.

At the library, while the other women are organizing the DVDs and preparing the coffee stand, while they are making change for the book sale and emptying the northwest corner of the building to make room for the computer lab that will go in next week, Genevieve is emptying the photo frame that sits on the long front desk. She removes the photo of her and her ex-husband, replacing it with a black backdrop. Then she slides in the scrap of paper and fits the glass face tightly on. As she adjusts the clamps and double checks they're firm, she looks up to see Avis and Mercedes standing in front of several empty shelves. It strikes her as something skeletal, and she is careful not to think of the day the entire library looks like this.

In their home on the other side of town, the Bronson parents are putting on their winter gear. Today is yet another anniversary of their daughter's death. They will go to the library and park in the middle of the road, their silent objection to the lack of stop sign before the crosswalk. They do this each year on this day. It is something meaningful, something political to make them forget her tiny frame lying there in the rain. It is something meaningful to convince them that no one is at fault.

When Avis sees the Bronsons' parked car, she consults her calendar to confirm the anniversary is today. Each year after she purchases her calendar, it is the first thing she records. She circles the date in red ink. The librarians look up when the first horn is honked from vehicles that must pass the parked car. The women flock to the large glass front doors and watch the traffic slither past.

In the car, Mrs. Bronson rubs her hands together and Mr. Bronson turns up the heat, then uncaps each of their coffees so they can start to cool. They are both thinking about what will happen to their ritual after the library is closed.

We are not unlike them, Mr. Bronson says, looking straight ahead. *The librarians, I mean.*

There is a symmetry, Mrs. Bronson replies. She pulls her hat farther over her ears and Mr. Bronson crosses his arms. *There is a symmetry,* she repeats, *in that they're responsible for inducing the end of the thing they made.*

Genevieve takes the frame to the wall where the photographer's hooks are aligned. She finds the last hook and places the small frame there, so that everyone can read the message, and come to understand the subtext of that which fills the wide wall.

The frame tells them, in the photographer's handwriting, that the exhibit is over.

V

LET X BE

THE DEATH OF A library is slow. Books are pulled from the shelves in an order like teeth leaving the mouth; it begins as perforation. Months pass this way, until standing on one end of the building you can see the opposite wall. Eventually, it earns the status of archiving nothing.

The photographer stacks the spoons one on top of another, places his chin on the table to study the uneven arcs.

She is touching them, too, fingering the cool dips, running her thumb along the back of the necks.

They sit at the kitchen table in opposing chairs; she looking at the back door, he looking at the stove. It is here, angled so they could see each other if they were still in the same world, that they are reduced, like an equation does with pattern or a photo with event.

And so they sit, together in ways, but also endlessly apart, holding the spoons, placing thumbs in the dips to feel the curve, noting the rust stains from oily fingers on the handles. They sit in their kitchen alone but together, placing one on top of another, aligning the coves just so, in order to learn what it means to reach a threshold. In order to discover the number of spoons possible to stack before they fall.

By the time the librarians remove the last of the books, the library is newly full. Each morning now people stream through the front doors with raised eyebrows and smacking lips, ready to access the world through keypad and screen.

On their way out one evening they see the Bronson parents standing at the crosswalk, not holding hands. The librarians cross the walk single file. When the Bronson parents see them they nod and Avis looks away. She thinks of the day the Bronson girl fell, her rush outside at the sound of the tires. She thinks of the tiny body lying there as a heap of bone and flesh and green corduroy dress. It was quickly evident there was nothing like life left, but she still kneeled, tried to determine where the front of the body was, the top. And then she heard the car door open and saw the people step out. Avis hasn't been this close to them since that scene years ago. She's watched them park and protest but avoided them when it came to the grocery store, post office, bar.

And here, now, she can't look.

Later, at the bar, they talk about everything except the library: their old lovers and the tricks to growing old, how best to remove stains, how often a will should be revised.

Avis isn't speaking, Mercedes notices, and she touches her arm. When a loud bout of laughter rises from Harriet and Genevieve, Mercedes whispers, *Don't worry. They couldn't look at us, either.*

The laughter dies and there is a long pause as the smiles on the women's faces dissipate.

That night, when Avis gets home, she opens the trunk of her car to remove the books she's saved, forgetting there aren't any left. As Avis peers into the empty space, rather than feeling pleasure that the mission is done, she is overwhelmed with the feeling that there is now nothing left to do. Just as she is pulling down the trunk lid, something catches her eye—a single book hidden in the far back of the empty space. She reaches for it but she can't extend long enough, and so she climbs inside the car's storage space.

It is a small volume, clothbound and dog-eared, the title of which is embossed. The spine is broken, writing riddles the margins, and inside the small envelope in the inside cover, a library card has been placed. The book contains a two-page epilogue.

Avis pulls out the card and notes the date, nods in agreement with the card. She holds it close to her and turns to enter her home, plans to place the book on the top left-most corner of her shelf. And this is how she forgets to close her trunk.

Therefore, and of course, in the morning, her car won't start. And so she has time to watch the local news, and learns that given the increase in traffic at the library, the county has confirmed plans to erect a stop sign at the crosswalk leading to the doors. There is no mention of the Bronson girl's sad end, the silent protests of her parents over the long and trying years.

When Avis turns off the television there is a snap and then the quick shrink of the image to a centered spot of white. And when the screen is black, blank, and waiting, she fully understands just what this means: everything is working toward resolve. They are each characters, she thinks, glancing at the title of the book she retrieved from her trunk, balancing on the edge of end.

WHEN A NEGATIVE FAILS, two worlds are evenly represented inside of one frame. The moment before the eye settles is one of possibility; oscillating between two images, the eye contests which narrative to follow, like a pendulum, where the difference is as slender and substantial as the breech between degree, between seeing the breath and not.

And then, exactly always, the eye resolves—

Since her death, the photographer takes only the elevator and waits so he can take it alone. He is done with angle, with ladders, ramps, and stairs. These are reminders of progress when for him everything holds still. How perfectly awful, he thinks, watching the blinking numbers above the door, to spend a lifetime asking for pose. Now it is all he knows.

When he finally reaches the top, the doors chime open and he is reminded of her empty shoes, her dirty clothes which he cannot wash. He hasn't made the bed, preserves the mark on the pillow where her head used to rest.

But now he is here and when he turns the corner, her office door greets him at the far end of the hall.

He sees a square of white in the center of her door, and as he approaches, the text coming into focus, memory slips through the pores of his mind and he realizes where he has heard it before.

Do you want to hear a joke?

he had read on her pad at the library that first day.

There were two answers he could have given. He had said yes. From the pocket in the back cover of the notepad she pulled a sheet of paper with the same words he reads here:

A physicist, a biologist, and a mathematician are sitting outside a downtown bar chatting and watching the busy street. They see two people enter an apartment opposite their table. After some time, three people emerge from the loft.
The physicist says that the measurement wasn't accurate.
The biologist claims that they have reproduced.
The mathematician: "If now exactly one person enters the building, it will be empty again."

His eyes start to glaze and he jabs absently for the keyhole, the key scoring marks in the wood. Then he stops, sinks to the floor, his back against the wall that stands between him and her proofs— her proof that the future splits.

From the other end of the hall, the image: him looking in profile out the window, elbows on his knees, the now-dark joke branded on her door, the empty frame where her name should be. It is all almost worthy of photograph.

Let X be a stack of spoons.

Let Y be the place where they become a pile.

WHAT IS RELATIVE IS scope. Along the borders of the empty library are cement sills filled with birds. In autumn they hit the glass windows, fall stunned, and collect. When winter is over, the preserved remains of dozens of birds line the building's margins. This is no less a frame than the plot of a story, the bones beneath her smile, the place where the photograph ends. Only that with a center can be emptied; the rest is simply damage.

One day the photographer wants to look at her spoons. He opens the drawer where she kept them and lifts the wooden tray but he hears one of them fall in the back. He reaches his fingers underneath the drawer to loosen the wheel's lock and pulls the drawer out, fishing for the spoon with his hand.

It is then that he feels it, the wicker basket hooked to the unit's back. And when his hands graze the spoon, he feels something else, too; cylindrical roles, without the tongue of film to tell him they are new.

Hours later he sits on the porch, drinking wine from a mug. There were thirty-three rolls in all, and already the stop bath is revealing what they hold; her, from all angles, her hands and feet and torso, her eyes and knees and legs. She, dressed in winter gear, in just her bathing suit bottoms or one of his flannel shirts, with her hair down or up or pinned halfway between. With her glasses, or without, fingers stained red from grading papers, or black from the marker they used on each other in bed, nails long and cropped short, painted and plain; with bangs and without. Her before scars and after, or while they're still stabs, with hair under her arms or the smooth dip, prime enough to lick; her, featured in autumn or fall, in the snow and rain, in front of their naked tree with thick mast and, too, before it was a seed, she with beer or wine, cut-off shorts or camisole, sockless, slippered, sandaled, shoed. Her feet and belly button. Her rear and her tongue. She, with a spoon in her mouth, on her nose, tucked behind her ear. She with all of the dirty words he wrote over the years, under her clothes, coiling around her form.

He polishes off the bottle quickly in order to return downstairs. He knows enough about angle to know that she didn't have another photographer in her life. It is a sadder story, he thinks, flipping on the light, descending the creaking stairs.

He knows enough about angle to know she took them herself.

WHAT IS LEFT IS condensation, sweat pills on her forehead, a wine glass, the mirror. Deposit is the ring of scum around the tub, the strands of hair between the boards, the fine web of memory lining the bed.

The photographer will come to spend his evenings filling the tub and then emptying it. He will do this each night: draw the bath, sit on the toilet lid, watch the tub fill, the steam coil around and through itself. Then, when full, he will clear the tub, study the water's twist and the drain's opening. When asked he will reply that this is meaning: emptying space, fingering the thick fissure left, filling it up again, as a mouth or room, as a cup or question. Love is adaptation, he will say; love is the study of change.

Sometimes in bed they would try to point out contradictions in idioms or phraseology, metaphors half dead so that people did not realize they were mixed. Once he wrote in black ink up her thigh, *Getting you off means turning you on*. Her language is now just a volume in the catalog of his knowledge, unused because it's unshared, as empty as a book shelved in a library for decades and never checked out. Lately he signs to himself in the mirror, but the only response is his echo in the wide span of the frame.

The photographer lights a cigarette. He stands on top of the closed toilet lid to lift the framed photo from the wall. He unclasps the back of the frame to remove the picture of the drowned book and replace it with his new print. He reaches his arm over the sink, where he ashes in the drain and glances at the corner of the room where a nest of her collected hair still lies.

She will fill his home again; he will shadowbox her proofs. At night, he will think of mixed metaphors, but will be careful not to talk. He always keeps an eye on his tongue.

THE PHOTOGRAPHER ENTERS THE library. He carries part of his exhibit underneath his arm; the rest of the frames, the librarians notice, are stacked in the rolling basket behind him. The librarians do not see him enter, are busy with patrons for the rest of the afternoon, answering questions like *Where do I click?*, fixing the coffee machine, and totaling fines for the DVDs. The librarians do not notice him come in and set up the exhibit, do not notice him lift the frame containing the deaf mathematician's lost bookmark from the wall and slip out the doors. It is only after Genevieve locks up that Harriet calls them from the far west wall. *Come here, and bring the liquor*, she says. Avis grabs two slender bottles from a shelf beneath the register.

As Avis walks toward the exhibit, she scans the wide corridor. It seems smaller without the books, she thinks, and imagines them lined up in neat rows in her living room. She uncaps a bottle and thinks briefly of the fate of those books after she's gone, distracts herself with a drink. Her colleagues are lined up in front of the exhibit, their heads at a tilt and their hands on their hips. The exhibit comes into focus and she stops abruptly. She takes another swig from her bottle and hands the other one to Harriet, who cracks the lid and drinks. Mercedes holds out her hand for Harriet's bottle and Avis passes hers to Genevieve, hitting her on the shoulder to break her gaze from the wall.

The frames are empty; only white stares back at them. And beneath each is a bit of text explicating the action absent from the photo above.

Captions, Genevieve says and takes another swig.

No, Harriet says, shaking her head at the ground. She rolls the bottle cap in her palm, and the thin aluminum clicks against her wedding ring. *Subtitles.*

There is another world, Avis thinks, in which he dies and she goes on living.

Look here, Mercedes says, *he named this one.*

Their lips move in unison as they silently mouth the words that hover above the photographer's exhibit.

THIS IS NOT SOUND

Figure 1

Underneath your smile is empty bone. It is cold enough to crack. You are looking up and it is snowing and your eyes are closed and your mouth is shut. I am concerning myself with your mouth. I want to fill every cavity, your thin gaps and dead tooth. I want to find your root, the square of it, the center, multiply by 0, void you, fill you up again.

Figure 2

It is not that death sits in corners, but is one, the meeting place of two flat lands. This is just your hand and a vacant wall, a hook. This is all different brands of empty; your hand a hand that does not hold a sound, your hand like breath or rest, the wall without a word. And I am caught here, trying to learn how to un your smell in the place beneath my eyes, how to non your taste in the space between my teeth.

Figure 3

This, your shadow on bright concrete, your black form on the street. This is a kind of you, but not, an un-you, non-you, ~~you~~. I cannot equate this with echo, having never heard your voice.

Figure 5

You are my prism, the glass body through which I pass;
you are my prison.

Figure 8

I have caught your reflection in the glass of a windowpane, in glass cradled by frame. Your bones are frame that let the lips shift. You frame the words through lip but don't let sound drift through your mouth. I never heard your voice but felt your breath and touched your teeth. Your teeth the bones that frame your black hole tongue.

Figure 13

This is how I equate your loss with lag: the blur of your face is a kind of delay, a decay of outlined form. If frame is construction, a brand of scaffolding, of structure and support from below, then it has a different meaning here, where it denotes end. Memory is a frame from which I am cutting you out, in which I am cutting you up and in half. Your body is only part here; it ends abruptly with frame. I have to imagine the other half rests now in verb, lives still in still life, not cut cleanly with sharp edge.

Figure 21

You are my addict. You are the empty space in my head, my attic.

Figure 34

This is maybe censored, black streaks from bad light. This is poor exposure, though blur is not a surrogate for mute. We are a negative. We need retouching.

Figure 55

You are sitting at the end of the bed, looking lost, sheets tossed in coil. There is nothing I would not undo for you—the bed, the past. You are my song in minor, in mirror. You are rough blankets I fold and am enfolded in. You sin. You syndrome of affection, breaking me into smile, grins splitting open my face.

Figure 89

This is your breath, your breast, both concerned with rest and air, with beat and bare. The skin of your chest will melt with time but not the bone. The bone is frame, like formula on which we build equation for which we find the X. The bone is where I am, the frame of this, my plot. The plot is where you are, both on the graph and in the ground.

Figure 144

Where does your lap go when you stand? Where does your fist go when you wave? Where does your smile go when you decay, when, after time and dark, the teeth the tongue the lip split and dissipate?

Figure 233

A differentiable manifold M is said to be parallelizable if the tangent vector bundle of M is trivial. A topological manifold M is said to be topologically parallelizable if the tangent microbundle of M is trivial. In some open set M in some Euclidean space R^n there exists a differentiable structure with respect to which the integral pontrijagin class p(M) of M is different from 1. On a topologically parallelizable manifold it is possible to have a differentiable structure with respect to which the manifold is not parallelizable.

Figure 377

If zero is empty, a gaping defined by frame, then so is your mouth.

MR. AND MRS. BRONSON are lying in bed.

Are you awake? she asks him.

Yes, he says.

Do you know the birds that collect on the library's windowsills? she asks.

Yes, he says.

Do you think they know what's coming just before they hit the glass?

He waits a moment. *No,* he says, and she reaches for him in the dark with her hand.

He holds her, feels her body shake beneath the sheets. Little time passes before she settles again.

Someone should write a book about that, she says.

WHICH IS THE SADDEST permutation?

A tub drains. A child falls. A library fills. A mouth splits.

A tub fills. A spoon drains. A man falls. A child ends.

The library is manned. The woman is spooned. The drain fills. The child voids.

The spoon falls. The mouth fills. The woman comes. The man goes.

The spoon falls. The mouth fills. The man goes. The woman comes.

A child ends. A tub drains. The end splits. The void fills.

THE AFTERNOON THE NEW stop sign is placed in front of the cross-walk, the women are told their time at the library is done. They do not object or debate. In ways they feel relieved. As they are getting ready to leave, they collect their things: paperwork and coffee mugs embossed with the library's name; frames with layers of photographs that have collected over the years. Avis takes down her calendar and Harriet grabs all the notepads with PUBLIC LI-BRARY branded on the top.

Genevieve stands in front of the children's section looking at ground zero. They painted over the animals she put up one summer a decade ago, replaced them with dark grey walls. The oak benches and tables are gone now, in their place chrome chairs so each child sits alone.

As Harriet and Genevieve head out the door, they tell Avis they'll see her at the bar. Avis waves without looking at them. She is studying the long list of lost books and finishing the last sips of a bottle.

When Avis meets up with the others at the bar, there are drinks waiting for them already and they all smile weakly at each other. They know this is the last time they'll drink together as librarians. From now on they will just be women who used to deal with books. From now on they'll be just their names: Harriet, Genevieve, Avis, Mercedes.

Did you see the front page of the newspaper this morning? Genevieve asks as the bartender brings them another round.

Library Saved! says Harriet, and they all shake their heads.

Do you think anyone even notices? Mercedes asks.

What, that we're gone? Avis replies.

No, Mercedes says, looking Avis in the eyes. *That there aren't any books inside.*

SHE STUDIED DIMENSIONLESS QUANTITIES for a few weeks one summer, numbers that do not correlate to the tactile properties of the world: ratios, decimals, fractions. But nothing you can touch comes in parts; things either are or are not. She abandoned dimensionless quantities when she realized she didn't want to spend her time underscoring the distance between things.

He would like to untake certain photos, like this one, her body floating in the tub, the dark words ascending her trunk. Or: he would like to crop it so that all you might see is the delicate hairs on her belly, how they grow darker around the vortex of her navel and the way it holds a bit of water like the hollow of a spoon.

Once she sat him down to explain how she understood the world. She told him X is the number of bones on a plate. He looked at her then, his forehead crimped with confusion. *But what if X isn't?* he asked.

EPILOGUE

A YOUNG MAN WALKS into a bar. He squints at the lighting, which is dim but much brighter than outside. He stamps his feet four times and brushes the snow from his coat. He smiles at the bartender, who waves at him, and reaches up to remove his hat but stops when he looks at the walls.

My god, he says loudly, *look at this!* He walks to the bar but doesn't consult the beer list, looks up and behind the long counter.

I haven't seen this many books in forever. I didn't even know collections like this still exist, he tells the ancient bartender who is wiping out mugs. *Where did they come from?* he asks.

Years ago some regulars donated them.

It's really an amazing sight, the young man says and sits himself down. He can't pull his eyes from the grandiose collection that stands on the wall in front of him. It stretches up until the books become just swatches of color. There is a large chunk of metal scaffolding with wheels, he notices, probably to retrieve them from the highest shelf. He is in such awe that he doesn't hear the bartender ask what he wants.

Sir? the bartender says.

Hmm? the man replies.

I'll give you a minute, the bartender says and smiles as he hobbles away, still wiping out the mug.

The young man stares for another moment or so. *Amazing, really,* he says. *I'll take an Old Fashioned,* he tells the bartender, who puts down his cloth. The bartender makes the drink as quickly as his aged hands allow and puts it in front of the man.

There you are, sir, and welcome to The Library.

The young man sips the drink tentatively, then takes a greater swallow. *Strange name for a bar,* he says, and the bartender smiles a bit.

Lots of people say that, the bartender says.

Strange word, "library," the young man says, and rolls his shoulders back, cocks his head to one side. *What does it mean?*

ACKNOWLEDGMENTS

My gratitude goes to:

Richard Powers, Alex Shakar, Ander Monson.

Michelle Dotter, Steve Gillis, Dan Wickett.

Ron, Valerie, and Leland Drager.

Allan G. Borst.